Praise for L. C. Rosen's *Lion's Legacy*

A New York Public Library Best Book of 2023
Booklist Editors' Choice 2023: Books for Youth

"Flirtatious friendships and a fun summer romance, Indiana Jones-esque booby traps, and the logistics of filming reality TV mesh seamlessly with heavier discussions of rightful ownership of historical artifacts, erasure of queer history, and the power of an actual apology. Rosen emphasizes the importance between connecting the historical existence and contributions of queer people to the queer community in the present and includes many small tidbits of queer history throughout. . . . [A]ction-packed and illuminative."

—*Booklist*, starred review

"*Lion's Legacy* by L. C. Rosen is a heart-pumping adventure filled with tributes to queer history and community as well as thoughtful discussions about the ethics of archaeology. This series opener is reminiscent of an Indiana Jones caper, with its near-death escapes, almost impossible puzzles, and dangerous bad guys. Rosen elevates his version with deft discussions about straight-washing, and encourages LGBTQ+ people to 'take back our history' and 'control the story.' Rosen delivers a mesmerizing mix of adrenaline-inducing escapades and queer legacy."

—*Shelf Awareness*, starred review

"Rosen has balanced a thrilling adventure with a flirtatious queer romance, while highlighting moments from history most won't learn about in school and discussing what responsible archaeology entails. While the magic rings are not real, the Sacred Band of Thebes was, and readers who enjoy Greek mythology and history will be riveted by this adventure. . . . A page-turning action-adventure that highlights the importance of reclaiming queer history and culture."

—*School Library Journal*

"This action-packed adventure inspired by history and legend engages in a conflict-driven exploration of the ethics of archaeology. Tennessee grapples with tangled emotions about his relationship with his father, his longing for community, and what it means to be in love. . . . An entertaining, emotional rush tackling critical subjects."

—*Kirkus Reviews*

"[G]ripping series kickoff from Rosen (*Lavender House*) that's both thrilling escapade and simmering romance. . . . Through Ten and Leo's visits to a museum of queer history and culture, and the meticulous detail with which the author recounts underreported events in Grecian history, Rosen makes an insistent case for recognizing and teaching LGBTQ history and understanding legacy."

—*Publishers Weekly*

"L. C. Rosen's *Lion's Legacy* is an entertaining queer adventure reminiscent of classic movies like *Raiders of the Lost Ark* and *The Mummy*. Firelit hidden chambers, puzzles with deadly stakes and a fun, casual romance hit all the essential blockbuster buttons in *Lion's Legacy*!

However, Rosen's take on the genre actively interrogates the ethics of treasure hunting, posing questions about the ownership of history and the responsible way to handle historical artifacts. . . . *Lion's Legacy* is a celebration of the strength of queer community, whether felt by two queer people passing on the street, or resounding through the uncountable queer lives that have intersected throughout history. Ten knows queer history can be fun, weird, tragic and beautiful, but above all he knows it's a history worth protecting."

—*BookPage*

"Rosen's delightfully adventurous romp puts a clever spin on Indiana Jones."

—*BuzzFeed*

"Step aside, Harrison Ford. There's a new Indiana Jones in town, and his name is Tennessee Russo."

—*Nerd Daily*

"Rosen's books are a treasure for teens who may feel like they have to placate others by toning down their identity."

—*Kveller*

"Rosen really embraces the best parts of pulp adventure, with fantastic puzzles, bad guys you love to hate, a dash of romance, and artifacts full of both wonder and hidden dangers. The narrative is also unabashedly queer: it frequently refers to how much queer history has been hidden or erased. . . . Ten doesn't have time for any of that revisionism—and neither does Rosen."

—*Paste Magazine*

"Dig into this book and find a new favorite hero. Tennessee Russo's quest for the Sacred Band of Thebes is lightning paced, thoughtfully nuanced, and powerfully queer. This is the very gay adventure you've been looking for—and the most fun you'll have reading a book all year."

—A. R. Capetta and Cory McCarthy,
bestselling authors of the Once & Future series

"Adventure has a new name, and it's Tennessee Russo! In this book of thrills and peril, Rosen invents a queer hero we deserve."

—Adam Sass, award-winning author of *Surrender Your Sons*
and *The 99 Boyfriends of Micah Summers*

"A thrilling and ingenious love letter to queer history, heroism, and community. In Tennessee Russo, Rosen gives us another unforgettable protagonist with heart, grit, and—most of all—pride."

—Caleb Roehrig, author of *White Rabbit*

"Lev Rosen has written a thrilling treasure hunt through queer history, told with wit, smarts, and heart. An inventive, unpredictable adventure that will excite and inspire teen explorers, historians, and romantics alike."

—Alex London, bestselling author of *Proxy*

KING'S LEGACY

KING'S LEGACY

L.C. ROSEN

U

**UNION
SQUARE
& CO.**

NEW YORK

**UNION
SQUARE
& CO.**

NEW YORK

UNION SQUARE & CO. and the distinctive Union Square & Co. logo are trademarks of Sterling Publishing Co., Inc.

Union Square & Co., LLC, is a subsidiary of Sterling Publishing Co., Inc.

ISBN 978-1-4549-4808-7 (hardcover)
ISBN 978-1-4549-4809-4 (e-book)
ISBN 978-1-4549-4810-0 (paperback)

Library of Congress Control Number: 2024951254

For information about custom editions, special sales, and premium purchases, please contact specialsales@unionsquareandco.com.

Printed in the United States of America

2 4 6 8 10 9 7 5 3 1

unionsquareandco.com

Cover and interior design by Marcie Lawrence

For Frank

Water surrounds us. It pours down from chutes lining the walls, cascading over archways in heavy blankets a foot thick. We could probably walk through it, but it would be hard, all that water pushing us to the ground. That would be okay if the archways didn't have spikes sticking out from the floor underneath them.

"What do you think?" Dad asks.

We're on a small island, one forgotten ages ago. Our research had brought us here, and sure enough, after pushing some rocks aside, we'd found an entrance to a tomb, a simple carved door leading down into darkness. We'd followed it down, looking for the treasure, and then, when we reached the bottom and gone through another set of doors, suddenly lanterns had flared, their paper screens long deteriorated, just stone and flame now. And then the door had fallen shut behind us.

There are three archways in front of us—left, right, and center—all covered by thick waterfalls over spikes that cut the water the same way they'll surely cut us. The water runs into the center of the room, where it flows down through a stone grate. The floor is wet but not flooding.

"Are you asking if I think we can walk over the spikes without getting hurt?" I call back. The water is loud, and we have to shout over it. "No! I think we'd be killed."

"It's just water, Tenny," Dad says, filming the room with his little camera. "We can get through water."

"It's a waterfall," I correct. "Strong enough to push us down. One slip and we'll be split in two."

"Well, let's look for some way to turn off the waterfalls, then," Dad says, taking out his flashlight. I do the same. The room is lit but not bright, so we don't see things until our beam shines directly over them—the carvings of samurai in the walls, the stone dragons wrapped around the top of each lantern, and, most important, the rings in the closed door behind us.

The pair of tall wooden doors is old but in good condition, painted with black lacquer that's kept the wood from rotting even with all this water. On each of the doors is a raised wooden circle. They're painted with intricate images that look jumbled. Inside each circle are more rings, getting smaller and smaller, nestled inside each other. Each ring spins independently. Whatever image was originally created when the circles line up correctly is now too mixed up to make out.

"I'll take the left, you take the right," Dad says, and we go to work spinning the rings on the two doors, trying to solve the puzzles.

I take out my own camera, filming with one hand as we work. The ring puzzles are harder than I thought they'd be at first—the image is complicated, almost pixelated, covered in colored squares smaller than my pinkie nail. Each one is traced in gold and a different color, and that's most of the inner rings, so I'm not even sure what I'm trying to arrange them into. I shake my head and look at the outermost ring instead. There's no border, nothing I can line it up with on the outside, but at least here I spot some features I can identify: an eye, a pearl. I think it's a dragon, the long snakelike type with a pearl under the chin that is traditional here in Japan. Knowing that makes it go a little easier. The next ring has the other eye, so I line them up. After that, it's all scales; the dragon is spiraling in on itself. It takes me what feels like ten minutes before I get the rings lined up, and then I spin them all carefully in unison, trying to find the position of the image. After a quarter turn, it clicks into place, the rings sinking farther into the door and becoming immobile.

"Got mine," I say, turning to Dad with a grin.

Then the ground starts to shake.

At first I think it's an earthquake, but then I look at the grate on the floor. It's closing—which means the gallons of water pouring in around us now have nowhere to go.

"Dad," I say, "we're going to drown."

Dad turns away from his puzzle. "There must be a trick," he says. "Maybe I need to finish mine or—Look!" He points at the archway on my side of the room. "The spikes are gone." He's right. The water is still crashing down, but the spikes are gone. We can safely pass through one of the archways.

Safe being relative. The water is already past my ankles.

Sometimes, when I get overwhelmed, it helps me to go through the options quickly:

1. Stay and help Dad with his puzzle, and hope solving it stops the water.
2. Go through the open archway alone, and hope something there stops the water.
3. Pull Dad through the open archway, leaving his puzzle unfinished. Better to drown together than alone, right?

"You go," Dad says, still shouting over the water. "I'll keep working on this one. Look for something to open the grate."

I stare at him a moment longer, not wanting to leave him as the room floods, but he's right, we need to split up. I tear off. Luckily my camera is waterproof, so as I push through the water falling from the arch, I don't need to worry about anything but dropping it. I was right about the water—it's heavy, hard to move through, pushing me down so I'm practically crawling through it. If the spikes had still been here, I'd be dead.

On the other side is a set of stairs up to a small platform. I climb the stairs, soaking wet now but glad to be slightly above the water, which is growing ever higher. I glance back through the arch, but I can't see Dad from here, just the water, churning, rising.

The platform is built into the wall, like a shelf with steps leading to it, but I don't find anything else once I'm up there. The walls are rough stone, and I don't see carvings or anything to indicate what to do next. Only the platform's floor looks at all interesting. It's wooden, decorated with a pattern like the ring puzzles but cut in half, the circle sliced down the middle. There's no way to turn the pieces into a different position.

"Got it!" I hear Dad shout over the water. But the water doesn't begin to drain like I'd hoped it would. "The other archway is safe now, Tenny!" Dad calls. "I'm going to go through it. Get out the walkies!"

I take my walkie-talkie out of my backpack. It's not one of those cheap plastic things; this is more like a short-range phone, waterproof, shockproof.

"Okay, there's some stairs to a platform," Dad says through the walkie-talkie. "But . . . nothing up here."

"Same here," I say. "The floor has a pattern, though." I glance behind me and see the water still rushing up toward my feet. It's high enough now that it's only a few steps down. If I went back into it, I'd have to swim.

"Yeah, there's a pattern on my floor, too. A half circle made of four half rings, like one of the door puzzles. What do you think yours shows?"

I look down at the pieces. I recognize some of the scale pattern. "Maybe a dragon? That's what my door puzzle was."

"Mine was a bunch of katanas," Dad says. "All in sheaths, one sort of in front of the rest, which were making a circle."

"The Misumune katana?" I ask. That's the treasure we're after.

"Probably. And the dragon is probably the one who gave it to Misumune, according to the legend."

"So, what is . . . ?" I look down at the half circle again. Some pieces are scaled, but others have longer lines, overlapping—like swords. "I think . . . some of these pieces don't belong."

"I was thinking the same thing. You think we need to switch them?"

"Yeah," I say, already stripping off my backpack. "You wait there. I'll swim over with mine."

"Be careful," Dad says.

"Just get the camera out," I say, kicking off my shoes and rolling off my socks. I'm sure the water is filled with bugs and maybe leeches, and it's not like I haven't already been drenched, but I also hate waterlogged shoes. We once got caught in a water trap in a Mayan temple, and afterward my shoes were soggy for what seemed like forever. It was gross. The less water in them, the better.

5

I pick out the two half rings that look like swords, not scales, and jump into the water, leaving my backpack, jacket, shoes and socks behind. The water isn't just pouring down at a high speed; it's rushing everywhere. I'm immediately pushed away from the archway and then into a corner, where the water ricochets me against one wall, then the other, until I drift back out toward where I jumped in. It's like a whirlpool. I kick hard and try pushing myself off a wall with my foot to get out of it, and I manage to get a little farther toward the archway. The pieces of the puzzle are light and wooden, and they float, which makes it easier to keep my head above the water but harder to actually swim, since they start to drift away and I have to grab them in both hands. I have to rely just on my legs.

I kick forward as hard as I can, my head bobbing above the water, but with all the splashing and churning, it's easy to lose sight of where I'm going. The water almost half fills the chamber, and at this rate, it'll be past the platform edge by the time I make it back. Will I be able to slot in the puzzle pieces if they're underwater?

I reach the arch into the main chamber, and grab the wall again, pulling myself through it, both pieces in one hand now. The force of the water pushes me under for a moment, but I hold my breath and keep using the wall to pull myself along until I can feel the pressure lighten. Then I pop up. I'm back in the central chamber, but one of the puzzle pieces I was carrying is now floating a foot away.

I kick off the wall and grab it. The water here is swirling, too, but it's more open and less forceful. The lanterns that hang from the ceiling cast a weird flickering light on the surface. I swim forward, my legs already burning, and reach the next archway, the one on Dad's side.

Again, I grab the wall and pull myself through it while underwater. My lungs ache from how much air I've been pumping in and out just swimming over here. Holding my breath for so long makes me feel like I'm going to burst, but when I can't stand it anymore and pop up through the surface, I'm through. Dad is waiting on his platform, filming me, but he stretches out a hand. I tread water, throwing him the two pieces one by one.

"Give me the dragon pieces!" I shout.

"Do you want me to swim back? You look tired."

"No, just put these in. There's no time." The water is just inches away from covering the platform. I don't think I'll make it back in time to assemble my puzzle on dry land.

Dad tosses two pieces into the water, and I grab them and immediately swim back. I need to go faster this time. I don't know if whatever mechanism this is will work when it's underwater.

The first waterfall pushes me under again, and this time I shove the puzzle pieces under my arms, going as low as I can, farther from the pressure of the falling water. Toward the bottom I can still feel it, but not as strongly. Even the currents pushing me around are weaker down here. I open my eyes. It's dark, but I can tell where to go. I swim underwater, and it's easier, faster. I pop up once for breath in the middle of the chamber, and then again right before the next archway. I take as big a breath as my ragged lungs will allow, then dive under again, pulling myself along the wall.

I'm definitely faster this time. Maybe I'll make it.

When I break the surface of the water on the other side of the waterfall, I'm greeted by one of my shoes floating on the surface. My heart, already racing, seems to stop. I look over at the platform—the water is about an inch over it. I'm too late.

"Tenny?" Dad calls through the walkie-talkie. "Tenny, are you okay?"

I kick myself over to the platform and use the stairs, now underwater, to pull myself up. The pieces I left are still in their slots, even under the water. I just need to force these two new pieces into their places. I hope this works.

I take the first piece and push it through the rising water, into the empty half ring space. And I feel it click. It will work! I take the other piece and do the same. I feel it click, too.

For a moment, nothing happens.

And then the room goes dead silent. It almost hurts, the sudden quiet. The water has stopped rushing in.

"Tenny!" Dad calls out, his voice clear now without the walkie-talkie.

"Yeah, Dad!" I call back, standing over the half circle. "We did it!"

There's a *thunk* and suddenly the water starts to drain away, quickly falling down from the platform and the stairs. I grab my floating shoe before it sinks with the water. It's not totally soaked, at least. My socks are, though. The water continues to drain as I put my shoes back on. When the ground is, well, not dry, but just regular wet stone, I climb down the steps and walk back into the main chamber. The spikes in front of the third central archway have lowered.

"Nice work," Dad says. He's filming the last of the water rushing down the reopened central drain but pans up to film me, grinning. "How was it compared to the Mayan temple?"

I tilt my head, thinking. "I didn't have to swim as far, but the currents were a lot stronger," I say, "and I took my shoes off this time."

"We gotta check for leeches," Dad says. "But first . . ." He points to the new archway. We go through it carefully and find a set of wet stone stairs leading up to a large wooden door. It pushes open easily. "It probably unlocked when the water shut off."

Inside is a large circular chamber that's shockingly warm. Lanterns hang from the ceiling at different heights, all of them flaring to life as we enter, thanks to some ancient mechanism. Small white ribbons, or maybe slips of paper, are tied around them in various places, drifting in the breeze that opening the door has created.

In the center of the room is a black stone cube with benches on each side of it. It's radiating heat. You can see heat coming off the cube, warping the air.

"You think . . . ?" Dad says.

"It's to dry off?" I finish.

"Yeah."

"Well." I shrug. "Let's take advantage then." I take my balled-up socks out of my pocket and lay them on one of the benches, and then do the same with my shoes, backpack, and jacket. Dad strips off everything, down to his boxers.

"Let's only film from the waist up, eh?" he says, sitting on one of the benches.

I don't love being in only my underwear with my dad, but my shirt and pants are already cold and clingy, so I take them off, too, and lay them on the benches before sitting down next to Dad.

"Just don't film me at all," I say.

He laughs. "Come on, I'm sure some guys out there would love to see you shirtless."

"Dad, ew."

He laughs again, then rifles through his backpack and takes out a granola bar. He motions me to film him. "Waist up," he says again. I make sure to not even show his nipples.

"While we're drying is a great time to replenish our energy," he says to the camera in that cringe advertising voice. "And QuickFix Granola Bars are what we use to keep our brains and muscles working while exploring ancient ruins like these."

He unwraps the granola bar and takes a bite, chewing thoughtfully. I film for a few seconds before lowering the camera.

"Really?" I ask.

"It's a good moment for it. We gotta wait to dry off. May as well use the time to get the plug in."

"I guess," I say, holding the camera up to him again as he eats.

"You want one?" he asks.

"Only if you promise not to film me eating it until my shirt is back on."

He chuckles and hands me one. "They're not bad, but they'd be better with chocolate chips instead of raisins."

I take it from him and try a bite. He's right; it would be better with chocolate. "Why is QuickFix our sponsor now?" I ask. "The Grizzled Foods ones were better."

Dad shrugs, but I see him look away, too, his face strange for a moment before it's shadowed. "Just didn't want them as our sponsor anymore," he says.

"After five years?" I ask.

"QuickFix made me a better deal."

"Better enough that we can buy our own chocolate chips and just add them?" I ask.

He snorts. "No." He gets quiet in a way he almost never does. In a way that means something is bothering him.

"What is it?" I ask.

He sighs. "Fifteen is hard," he says suddenly. "I want to keep protecting you, but you're also almost an adult now, and I want you to know what the world is like."

"Dad, we're literally eating granola bars in an ancient tomb after escaping a flood trap that almost drowned us. What does 'protect' even mean in this situation?"

He laughs, then frowns. "Yeah . . . okay. So . . . I asked QuickFix to sponsor us after Grizzled dropped us."

"They dropped us?" I ask, surprised. Dad had been eating their stuff on the show for years.

"After last season. They . . . weren't interested in being affiliated with us anymore."

"Okay . . . ," I say, confused, until it hits me a moment later. "Because I came out."

Dad flinches but nods. "They said it doesn't mesh with their brand."

The granola bar is tasteless in my mouth, but I chew and swallow it anyway. "Okay."

"I'm sorry." He scoots closer. "I don't know if I should have told you. But . . ."

"No," I say. "I'm glad you did. I want to understand this stuff." I look up at the large heating cube. The air around it is wavering. "But I'm sorry if—"

"No," Dad interrupts. "You don't apologize. They're a homophobic company, and I'm glad we're not shilling for them anymore. If I could, I'd go back and cut them from all the other seasons. They don't want my son? I don't want them. But I'm sorry that the world . . . is like that."

I smile and lean my head on his shoulder. "That's okay, Dad. You're not responsible for the whole world. Just for me. And for keeping me from drowning."

He grabs me around the shoulders, giving me a squeeze. "Okay, I feel pretty dry now. You?"

"Yeah," I say. I stand and check my clothes. They're mostly dry. Except my shoes, of course. We get dressed again. My shirt smells like hot stone and moss. My clothes are toasty warm, like a hug. So what if some trail mix company doesn't want me selling their stuff because I'm queer, right? I'm still going on adventures they wish they could have.

"This is quite a setup," Dad says, buttoning his shirt. "I guess next is . . ." He points at a door at the far end of the room. I pick up the camera. We cross the room and open the door. Beyond is a long hallway lined with . . .

"Skeletons," Dad says. "Creepy. Hope they don't come to life."

TWO YEARS LATER

❧ ONE ❧

I've done more difficult things than this before. I've evaded traps, run away from magically reanimated skeletons, found lost treasures, become kind of famous, and survived all of that. So I should be able to handle a task that many would consider simple. And yet it's like my hands won't do what they should. They freeze up and cramp, bending wrong, pulling too hard, and—

The wrapping paper tears again. I sigh.

"Just use a gift bag," my mom says behind me. "We have dozens in the closet."

"I thought it would be funnier wrapped," I say, looking down at the motorcycle helmet I bought Gabe for his birthday. He just got his license, and he might not have an actual motorcycle yet, but I want to make sure that, once he does have one, he doesn't hop on it unprotected. Gabe can run ahead without thinking too much. He's my best friend, and sometimes a bit more than that, so I'm not being shady or anything. He'll like it, because it's the kind of thing he knows he should think about but might forget in his excitement.

I go to the closet and fish out a huge pink gift bag. It looks like it was for a baby shower or something. It's got glittery satin handles, and the pink is patterned with rattles. It's perfect. I put the motorcycle helmet inside. Mom snorts a laugh when she sees it.

"It matches," she says. She's right. The helmet I got him is neon pink with lightning bolts down the sides. Kind of punk-princess-genderfuck vibes. Just like Gabe.

"It's a theme," I say.

"If you stay over, let me know," Mom says.

"I will."

"And you really have to pack tomorrow. I don't want you rushing to the airport because you had to throw your underwear in your bag at the last minute."

"I don't leave for, like, three days," I say.

"Still."

"Yeah, fine," I say, giving her a kiss on the cheek. "See you later."

She smiles and waves goodbye at me. "Tell him happy birthday for me."

"I will."

I leave the apartment and head out into the city. I love New York in the summer. It bakes you like an oven and smells like warm piss, but people go kind of nuts in the best way. Parks crowd over like sold-out music festivals, with people having picnics, drinking wine in public, playing Frisbee. There are dogs everywhere. I swear, everyone gets a new puppy in June. And the queers like me? We go wild. Tank tops with arm holes that hang below our waists, so you can see every inch of our stomachs. The shortest possible shorts you can find. You can always spot a gay picnic in the park, because at least one person is in a speedo even though there's no beach or pool. The rest of the year, we can still spot each other, but in summer, everyone can see us. It's like we put up big flashing lights saying QUEER and challenge anyone to give us shit for it. I love it. It makes sense that Pride is in June.

I was actually asked to be on one of the floats for the parade this year. Some new Internet startup for selling houses. I said no, because Pride is way too corporate now, and I don't want to add to that, but then the Queer Historians of New York said they were marching and asked me to march with them. It's not a float, but I'm really excited for it, even though it's a month away. And they were happy I said yes. I'm not *famous-famous*, but since the last season of the show aired, I've gotten . . . gay famous? There are memes of me, mostly nice ones, taken from the show. I never really used social media that much before—I just posted photos of friends and stuff—but after last season aired, I went from a few thousand followers on Instagram and TikTok to over a hundred thousand on each. TikTok checkmarked me without asking. So I started using it, posting about queer history, sometimes some behind-the-scenes stuff about the show. I especially love the history videos I do on TikTok. And people comment all the time. I've stopped looking, 'cause it gets weird—women my mother's age telling me I'm cute, people asking for photos of me and Gabe kissing or commenting "love is love," and rainbow emojis under every post, including the one about Nero. And, of course, angry, nasty people telling me I'm perverting history and lying, that I have an agenda. A few real historical questions, too. I wish I could weed out the good, but it was all too much, so I just stopped looking. But the comments still come on every photo and video I post.

I take a photo now of the sun setting through the buildings. Gabe's family is in Tribeca, so I'm going to get on the train in a second, but for now the city is painted pink in the light, the buildings are glowing, and a shirtless guy in jean cutoffs so short they may as well be underwear is roller-skating by. I snap a photo, making sure I don't get his face, and post it: *I love the city in summer.*

Nine likes, immediately. But one is from my dad. I smile, then put my phone away before I start seeing the comments. I like being able to post photos. I like knowing Dad sees them. Everyone else I can ignore. But with him always running around the globe, doing research for the show, I feel like social media is a way to keep showing him my life without just, like, texting him random photos. That would be weird. We're good now, but maybe not *that* good. Still, after our heart-to-heart when we found the wedding rings of the Sacred Band of Thebes, he's opened up a lot. We email all the time, and we talk about stuff, like the ethics of what we do and where artifacts belong. Do you return treasures of minority peoples to the governments they live in when you know that government will destroy them? Whose story are you telling? He's really interested in it now—in being a better person, not just a better dad.

I head down the stairs and into the station. The subway especially smells like piss in the summer, but you get used to it. I make sure to get on a car with working air-conditioning and take out my phone again, going over some research notes for the next season of the show. Since the last season did so well, Dad got an offer to move the show to a big streaming network and took it. It means a bigger audience, which means more people will learn about queer history, which I'm so excited about. There's a new marketing push, too, apparently.

I don't understand that side of it, exactly—Dad handles it—but I know it means the pressure is on for the next season to be even better. But even with all that, Dad says I'm still in charge of what artifacts we go after. It's important to him that we do this together, and that means I get to make some of the bigger choices.

The problem is, you never know what's going to be an adventure. Dad has a nose for it; he can, like, sense if something is going to be big, if there are going to be hidden temples and traps and all that. But I don't have that. So I've been throwing out history I'm interested in—queer history—and seeing what he thinks. I do research, suggest an object or a place, and then he flies to the location and looks around, sees if he gets whatever feeling it is that tells him there's something there, and hunts for any leads. And since I still have school, we have to time filming around that, which means our next season has to film this summer.

Dad says the tomb of Oscar Wilde might be good—a literal wizard spoke at the dedication, there was a piece removed from it, it was built in secret—but he doesn't sound too enthused. I don't know if that's because the vibe just isn't that strong or the history isn't that old or what. I haven't asked. I'm afraid he might say he doesn't want to do two queer seasons in a row. And that's not fair of me, I know. Dad and I have had our issues, and he hasn't always been the best person, but he's always been great about me being queer. So I don't know why I feel that way. But I do. Like I'm turning everything gay.

Which is just what those nasty comments tell me I'm doing, I realize. I shake my head as I get off the train. I'm not turning anything gay. They were already gay—I'm just showing that to the world. Every season should be gayer than the last, just for the people who can't see that.

Gabe's family lives in a cool loft on Canal Street. It's one of those buildings that hasn't been totally modernized and still has a crank elevator. Gabe had to show me how to use it when I first came over. I pull the crank and watch the walls roll by as I rise into the air. I stop at the seventh floor, where the door to Gabe's apartment is already open. Gabe is standing there grinning. He's wearing one of those tank tops with the arm holes, his dark skin visible all the way down the sides, and his fro-hawk is a faded pink from the bright red he dyed it a few months ago. It matches the helmet.

"Happy birthday!" I say, giving him a hug. He grabs me tight, lifting me up in the air. He puts me down and pecks me on the lips, which is how he greets all his close friends, then takes the bag from me.

"What did you get me? I said no presents."

"Yeah, but . . . ," I say.

He's already pulling the helmet out, eyes wide. "Yes!" he says. "This is amazing." He hugs me again. "Thank you."

"You're welcome," I say, happy he likes it. We walk into the apartment. It's an open floor plan with lots of light from the street, and all the old metalwork is still visible. His parents are artists—well, his dad is an artist; his mom is an art dealer. His dad was really big in the '80s, and the whole apartment still feels like the '80s—there's spray paint on the concrete wall, the rug is neon purple, and the furniture is black. It's funny, because it kind of matches Gabe perfectly, but then his parents come around the corner. His mom is in a very chic black bodycon dress with a nearly shaved head and long dangling earrings, and his dad is in a deep green suit, his tight natural curls almost entirely gray.

"Hi, Ten." His mom smiles warmly. "I'm glad Gabe wants some company on his birthday. I told him seventeen should be a party, but he said he just wanted to order Chinese food and watch bad movies with you."

"Everyone is already gone for the summer," Gabe says with a shrug. "And besides, who wants to have a party with their parents' permission?"

His dad laughs and turns to his mom. "We said we'd be cool parents, parents who let their kids do what they want to do as long as it's safe, and then he begs us for rules so he can break them."

"Like father like son," his mom says, kissing his dad on the cheek. "Well, come on. If we're more than an hour late, Joan is going to give me an earful. Make sure he shows you the guitar we got him, Ten."

My eyes widen expectantly. Gabe is a musical prodigy—plays guitar, flute, bass, all expertly. The flute he picked up without lessons when he was ten and just figured out. He says he doesn't have a favorite, though, and really wants to be a composer more than a musician, so I don't, like, pressure him to start a band with me. Though that would be very cool. Especially if we called it Queer Historians. I haven't doodled out a logo or anything.

"All right, happy birthday again, son," his dad says, squeezing Gabe into a hug. His mom kisses him, and they head out the door.

Gabe turns to me, smiling, still holding the helmet. He puts it on. It looks disproportionate on him, the black tank top and torn jeans suddenly seeming much narrower, even though he's not especially narrow.

"It looks good on you," I say.

"Is it weird that I kind of want a blow job while I'm wearing it and nothing else?"

I laugh. "It's your birthday, so if that's the fetish you want to develop, I'm happy to help."

He laughs, then flips up the visor. "Maybe in a bit." He grins and takes the helmet off, but then bites his lower lip. "Actually . . . there's something else I was hoping you'd give me."

I raise an eyebrow. "Wait, is there really like a weird kink you want to—"

"No!" he interrupts, then laughs. "I mean . . . I don't know. I don't think so. But no, I'm not talking about sex. I . . ." He sighs. "I want to go with you to Paris. For the tomb. I want to go on an adventure with you. Just watching last season, it was so cool, and I—"

"Yeah," I say. I'm surprised but not that surprised. He asked me a lot of questions while last season was airing. He loved the stories, and he's always been a thrill seeker, so I kind of figured he might ask at some point.

"Yeah?"

"I mean, I need my dad to say okay, and then we need your parents to say okay, and then maybe because there's this new network, the new producers would need to okay it, and there's paperwork—"

"Oh, I did all that."

"What?" That doesn't make sense.

"Your new producer. She called me up—she's the one who asked me to go with you. I mean, I wanted to anyway, but I thought maybe it was going to be too complicated, but when she asked me, I asked my parents. They're cool with it. They love the idea of me going to Paris, and I think they think it's mostly fake, or at least that there's no way you'll find two deadly temples in a row. So . . . I just need your okay. And your dad's. But I mean, I really don't want you to say yes just to say yes. If I'm going to be in the way . . ."

"New producer?" I frown. I know we have them, but I haven't spoken to any. Why are they talking to Gabe?

"Yeah. She said because of our social media popularity and how people like the photos of us together that I sometimes put up and think we're a couple and stuff, it would be good for the show?" He frowns. "I know, I know, it's not like . . . a great reason. But I figured if that means they want me to come too, I should just go with it. That okay?"

I tilt my head, thinking.

"Oh no, it's not, is it? I'm sorry, Ten, I can tell her I won't—"

"No," I interrupt. "I love the idea of you coming. I just don't know this producer or what her agenda is. It's weird she didn't talk to me first, right?"

"She said she just thought it would make good TV. She originally wanted me to surprise you at the airport, but I said that wasn't cool."

"Huh," I say. I take a breath. "Okay, well, I'll figure her out later, but you get to come!" I grin widely. I do love that. I love the idea of being able to bring him and have an adventure buddy, like I did before with Leo. And I didn't even know Leo before, but now he's one of my closest friends, or at least as close as we can be since he still lives in Greece. Going in with someone who's already a friend sounds like fun. And it's sometimes good to have a buffer with Dad around.

"I get to come!" Gabe grabs my hands and jumps up and down.

"Oh wait, my dad," I say. "He needs to okay it." I take out my phone and dial him.

"Isn't it late?" Gabe asks.

"It's seven, so in Paris it's like midnight . . ." I frown. "Maybe a little. But he just liked a post on Instagram, so he's awake."

"Tenny!" Dad says as he picks up. "I was going to call you. I have news."

"Okay," I say, "but first I need to ask if Gabe can come to Paris with us. His parents say it's okay, and apparently some new producer told him he should come. Do you know her or—"

"Yeah, sure, of course Gabe can come. But, Tenny, here's the thing: we're not going to Paris."

"What?"

"You didn't see the news today? The big find?"

"I . . . no," I say. I hadn't checked any archaeological news sites today. I was mostly just researching Wilde . . . and then spending hours trying to wrap Gabe's helmet.

"They found evidence of the lyre in Jerusalem. I'm there. I just looked everything over. It's for real, Tenny. The lyre from the legends was here. And it was taken to Rome. I'm just rearranging all your tickets. We gotta move fast, though, so your new flight is tomorrow morning, okay?"

"Wait, what?" I feel my whole body kick-start, a *thunk* like my motor just revved up. We're starting.

"The lyre, Tenny. King David's lyre. The one Jonathan gave him. It's real, it was here, and it was looted during the Crusades and lost to time after that. But we're going to find it."

⚜ TWO ⚜

I take a deep breath, my eyes focused on Gabe, who looks confused. The phone is still pressed to my ear.

The lyre Jonathan gave King David. It was one of the things I'd found in all my research, something I'd shown Dad. It was mentioned in just a few records. A gift Jonathan, son of King Saul, gave David—a lyre he hand-carved and strung, and which David then played only for Jonathan. Jonathan, his lover. A lot of people disagree on that point. After all, these are ancient figures in the Torah, the Bible. No way they were queer, right? Except they were. And not just because of their solemn promise to be *best friends*—as it's been interpreted—or because Jonathan "knit himself to the soul of David" and stripped naked to make a covenant with him—that's all just symbolic according to straight people. Doesn't seem like the usual way to proclaim friendship to me, at least not the kind of friendship in which you don't have sex, but that wasn't what convinced me.

No, the thing that proved it to me was the word used to describe their love. Jonathan and David loved each other. There are a lot of words for love in Hebrew. Love between parents and children, between a king and his people, between siblings. But the word used for Jonathan and David's love is used in only two other places: the love people have for god, and the love between husbands and wives. Jonathan and David may have had wives, but they were lovers, too. They were queer. I'm sure of it. And centuries of straight people rewriting history just erased that.

"Okay," I tell Dad, my eyes wide. "We're going to find the lyre!" My voice goes up a little at the end, and I blush.

"I'll make sure Gabe has tickets, too. I'll meet you in Rome. Go pack."

"Okay," I say again. Dad hangs up, and I stare at Gabe, my mouth still open in shock at how fast it's all happening.

"What's going on?" Gabe asks. "Can I come?"

"Yes," I say, grinning. "But we're not going to Paris. We're going to Rome. To find King David's lyre."

"Who?"

"King David. From the Bible."

"Like David and Goliath?"

I nod.

"He was queer?"

"Yeah, I mean . . . people say no, but there's evidence he was. It's in the text."

"Okay, well . . . I'm still coming, though?"

"Yes. Dad is getting our plane tickets right now. But . . . we gotta leave tomorrow."

"Tomorrow? I guess that means I have to pack now. No time for bad movies."

"Sorry to cut your birthday short. I should probably head home soon."

"Yeah." He nods, then grins, wicked. "Though if you want to try that thing with the helmet . . ." He wiggles his eyebrows.

"Well, I guess it is your birthday."

The next morning, I meet Gabe at the gate for our flight to Rome. He's reading about King David and Jonathan on his phone.

"It says they wrote each other poetry," he says when I sit down next to him. "Why don't I know any of this?"

"Queer history, especially of biblical figures, isn't usually taught in school. Too controversial. People get really angry."

"Yeah, I know. I used to look at the comments when you tagged me in photos."

"Sorry about that."

I am genuinely sorry. With me, the bad comments are homophobia, and sometimes antisemitism if I mention being Jewish; most people assume I'm Christian because my dad is. But with Gabe it's always racism. Even when there's no homophobia, even when the commentor is gay or says something about loving gay people. Being Black and gay and even close to the public eye is brutal, so now I only post photos of Gabe with his okay, and I never tag him.

"No worries," Gabe says. "My accounts are all anonymous for a reason. But you need yours public to talk about history, so that's the price of fame, right? Although, I guess you could stop posting everything else—personal photos . . . You could have a different account for that. My dad always says it's good to be known by what you do, not who you are."

I shrug and sip from my water bottle, which I filled at a fountain. "Yeah, but . . . I want people to see all of me. Or . . . more than just lectures. Like . . . if I think about how people will remember me in the future, *if* they do, then I want to give those historians a full picture. Make their jobs easy—more information, less guesswork."

He laughs. "And for me, it's a relief that people don't really know me."

"Well, get ready." I pull my backpack onto my lap. "After this season, you'll be even more famous."

He frowns, then tilts his head, considering. I watch different things flash over his face—maybe the realization of what he's doing, how much more public he'll become, and how dangerous that could be. But there's something else, too. An eagerness that's more than just his usual hunger for thrills. "But I get to have an adventure with you! So I'll just keep my accounts private. And definitely won't read the comments."

"That's smart," I say, hugging my bag. "I wish I could, but, like, there are so many queer kids out there who follow me and say nice things, too. I don't want to close them out. Just the assholes."

"Yeah," Gabe says, taking my hand. "Those kids are lucky."

I'm about to ask him more about why he wants to come along, about why he wants this adventure, about that look on his face, but then—

"Oh my god, you two are so cute," says a woman suddenly standing in front of us. She takes out her phone and snaps a photo without asking if I'm okay with it. "Adorable."

"Hey," I say, "could you not? I didn't give permission to have my photo taken."

"Oh, like that matters," she says, rolling her eyes. "But, actually, you did. In your contract. We have permission to use your image for promotional purposes for the show, and that means I get to take your photo!"

"What?" I ask. "'We'?"

"Oh, riiiiight." She shakes her head like she's a funny, ditzy sitcom character. "Sorry, sorry. I've talked with your dad so many times, and I follow you on all the socials, and I've watched last season like three times, so I forgot you don't know me, even if I know you. I'm Sterling! Your new producer and camerawoman extraordinaire!" She grins, wide and fake.

I look her over. She's white, older than me, but not old as Dad, maybe in her thirties, and her blond hair falls to her shoulders, where it's curled a little, and the ends are pink. She's got black cat-eyed glasses, a black leather moto jacket, skinny jeans, and a white tee. Her wheelie bag is bright purple. I frown. Wheeled bags aren't great for adventuring. To get to the hotel, sure, but a backpack is better for running around.

"Camera equipment," she says, catching my stare. "Special case, foam inserts. I'm not trusting it to luggage handlers, though. I should have had a whole team, you know. Camera people, lighting, sound, but your dad said no to that, said it would make traveling fast impossible."

"Okay," I say. "That does sound like him, and he's right—but I'm going to check this out with him."

"She sounds like who I talked to," Gabe says, nodding at Sterling as I call my dad.

"Hey! You at the airport?" Dad asks. "I think a bunch of people are going to be looking for this lyre."

"Yeah. There's a woman here saying she's our new camerawoman and producer?"

"Yes! Well . . . maybe. What's she look like?"

"Thirties or forties?" I ask, looking Sterling over, who crosses her arms when I say "forties." "Pink hair tips?"

"That's Sterling!" Dad says. "Sorry, forgot to tell you. The new network insisted we bring someone along so the camera isn't as shaky. We've FaceTimed once or twice. She seems all right. Knows her stuff. Wanted me to wear foundation, though. So maybe she doesn't realize what she's in for."

"All right," I say. "I'll see you soon."

"I'll meet you at the airport. Try to sleep on the plane; we're going to head out right away."

"Okay."

I hang up and look at Sterling, whose eyebrows are raised, waiting.

"Nice to meet you," I say.

"You too!" She sits down next to me and I catch a whiff of peppermint. "I'm so excited to be on this show. I think since you came back last season, we have a real angle to work with. Like, your dad is great for the academics and the Gen X crowd, but a younger audience, millennial, Gen Z, they are *so* into this LGBTQ-plus stuff that it makes the archaeology thing new. Like, this isn't just some guy in temples with old stuff. This is the history of people that's been erased."

"You could do that with people of color, too," Gabe says.

"Right," Sterling says, still smiling. "But, honestly, then we'd lose some advertisers. Love Is Love is a great brand, but BLM is more . . . controversial."

Gabe stares at me, and I stare back, our eyes wide.

"Wow, really saying the quiet part out loud," Gabe says. "What if we were going after the history of trans folks?"

"Yeah, that wouldn't be great for the network either. Cis white gays are what sells." She shrugs but doesn't look apologetic. "Look, it's not like I like it. But my job is to manage the brand and make sure our sponsors are happy."

"Well, I don't think of the show as a brand, exactly," I say carefully. "This is history. And I like researching queer history because it's mine. Dad wanted me back, and he said I get to pick what we go after. This is what I'm interested in and feel like I should be bringing to light. I'd love to get into the history of queer cultures of color, or trans history, but I think then I would want a queer person of color or trans person to be a part of—"

"Right, sure." Sterling waves me off. "I get it. You love it. But it is a brand, whether you want it to be or not. A brand is what gets advertisers, and advertisers pay for marketing, and that means more people who watch and more people who learn about this history and stuff. Which is what you want, right? So let me handle the branding. In fact, let's go over your socials. I saw you don't have a Snapchat, and we need to get you one, stat."

"I have my Instagram," I say, but she keeps talking.

"And the history videos are great, but you could do more with your TikTok—what about all those couple challenges?"

"We're not a couple," Gabe says.

"What?" She laughs. "Yes you are. You're so cute together."

"We're best friends," I say. I don't add that, sure, sometimes we have sex. But Gabe doesn't want to be tied into something, and honestly, with the show, neither do I. My last boyfriend, one of the Good Upstanding Queers, as they call themselves, cheated on me. And then I had this amazing fling with Leo in Greece that we knew was going to end when I went home. And what I realized is that I like cuddling, and I like sex, sure, but I don't want a boyfriend. Last time I made having a boyfriend my whole personality, like it was my only connection to my queerness. The only history I could make. I don't want to get wrapped up in that again, and Gabe gets that. So we're best friends. No rules, and no jealousy. Like, I know Gabe has made out with some other guys, and, knowing he wasn't my boyfriend, it didn't bother me. I love Gabe, but I'm not in love with him. When we make out or sleep together, it's not romantic. It's fun. And that's been working really well for me. Because I get to focus on finding my queerness . . . without it being in another person. And I get all the benefits of both having the most amazing friend in the world and sleeping with a really good kisser.

"What? No." Sterling takes out her phone, her smile dropping for the first time, and starts scrolling through Instagram. "See?" She holds up a photo I posted a while ago, one of Gabe kissing me on the cheek, close to the lips, as I laughed because he was also surprise-tickling me at the time. "Did you break up?"

"I kiss my friends," Gabe says. "Do you not kiss your friends?"

"Not like that," she says, making it sound dirty somehow.

"So you're straight, then," Gabe says, smiling.

"I feel like that's supposed to be a dig, but yes, I'm straight," she says, tucking her hair behind her ears. "But I love you queers so much. That's why I wanted on this show. And because you two are so cute. C'mon, snuggle up." She leans back, holding her phone to take a photo.

Gabe and I don't move.

She sighs. "Fine." She puts the phone away. "But really, your cuteness and coupledom are part of the appeal right now, so don't go, like, announcing the breakup on socials, okay?"

"We didn't break up because we were never together," I say. "Is no sound coming out when I speak?"

"Huh?" She looks at me, confused, and I shake my head. I don't like this at all.

"Okay, well, we're going to go over more research on the lyre now," I say, taking out my own phone. "I can talk about that for the camera if you want."

"Yeah . . ." She tilts her head. "Yeah, sure, okay, that's part of the formula. And I don't know anything about what this lyre is, honestly. Your dad just texted last night and was like, 'New plan!,' but I just go with it, you know? Follow the talent's lead."

"Sure," I say. I look around for a seat, find one with just a window behind it, no people, and sit down in it.

Gabe comes over but stands with Sterling, looking at me. He grins. "I get to see this happen!" he says.

Sterling opens up her wheelie bag and gets out her camera. It's a nice one, but it looks too unwieldy for running around, and heavy, too. I hope she has others. If she doesn't, I do, at least. Small waterproof ones. The kind that have always worked fine before. She points the camera at me, and when I see the little green light go on, I smile and turn on the charm.

"So we're going for the lyre that Jonathan gave King David," I say. "You might not think that's queer history, but it is. People always try to act like queer people weren't in the Torah or Bible, but—"

"Wait." Sterling lets the camera slump. "The Bible? You're making the Bible gay now?"

"I'm not making anything gay," I say, trying to keep my expression cheerful in case she's still recording for audio. "It always was. I'm just not participating in erasing that queerness. I'm not making it straight. That's what most people do."

She blinks a few times. "Okay, look, you're right, and I agree with you, but I just want to say that this could be a little . . . controversial. Like, ancient Greeks, sure, everyone knows they were kinda gay. And Oscar Wilde? Yes, no problem. But the Bible?"

"Not the *whole* Bible," Gabe says. I smirk.

"Still," she says. "People aren't going to like this. This isn't good for advertising. Maybe we can change our flights?"

"We get to choose the artifact," I say. "I read the contract."

She frowns. "I guess you do, but is there anything I can say to convince you this is a bad idea? I mean . . . surely you can't really prove they were gay, right? We'd know about it, then."

"No, we wouldn't," I say. "That's the point. Hold up your camera, and I'll tell you the queer history, though."

She sighs and puts the camera back up. The green light goes back on, and while we wait for our flight, I talk. I talk about the word for love, *ahava*, and how Jonathan's dad was so keen to get David married but hated David, too, and tried to get rid of him. But Jonathan went to David because, according to the Hebrew text, he felt *chafetz* for David—desire—although *chafetz* is usually translated as "care for" or "like." I go through the books, starting with Tom Horner's, and explain how people have thought this since Stonewall, and probably way before. I bring up art on my phone depicting Jonathan and David, art that shows them looking like romantic partners in love: a French illuminated manuscript from 1290, a Goez illustration from the 1700s, a Victorian stained glass window from Edinburgh. This idea has been present for centuries. Everyone keeps seeing it even as everyone tries to deny it. David and Jonathan are a love story.

And when I'm done explaining all that to the camera, I smile and say, "And that's why it's queer history. This lyre was a love token. A gay one. And we're going to find it."

I wait for the little green light to turn off. I'm done. But instead Sterling keeps filming.

"So what would you say to devout Christians who think what you're saying is a lie?" she asks.

"I'd tell them to do the research themselves. And that if they want to keep believing Jonathan and David were just close friends who got naked and wrote each other romantic poetry, then I'm not going to stop them from thinking it. But this is my history, no matter how much they want to deny it."

"So you don't hate Christians?"

"What?" I ask, confused. "No."

"Can you say it as a sentence?"

"I don't . . . hate Christians?" I say.

"Not a question," she says, her mouth still in that fake grin. It must ache. "Just say it."

"Why?"

"Because if we edit it so that's at the top, people won't feel attacked."

"I'm not attacking Christians," I say. "I'm just talking about my history."

"I know that, but for advertisers ... y'know, sometimes new information can feel like an attack. Look, it's dumb, I get it, but we're talking about packaging, about image. We don't just want you saying, 'The Bible is gay,' without acknowledging that some people might be offended by that."

"I don't care if they're offended," I say, still confused, "because that's about them, not me. And it's definitely not about the history."

She takes a deep breath, the smile straining. "Can you please just say it?" Her voice is still perky, but it's fraying.

Sometimes, when my brain starts to overflow with possibilities, it helps to make a list of choices in my mind.

1. I can just do what she asks, say, "I don't hate Christians," and have her edit it into the top of the explanation. What could it hurt?

2. I can outright refuse, but based on her rictus grin, she might be able to just stare me down, waiting.

3. I can turn to Gabe for some idea, but he's just looking at me, waiting to see what I'll do. Though that doesn't mean I can't use him.

"Gabe," I say, and pat the seat next to me. He looks confused but sits down. I turn back to the camera. "Some of you might know my good friend Gabe from my social media. He's coming with us for this adventure. Gabe, what do you think about everything I just said?"

Gabe raises his eyebrows and grins, then turns to the camera. "It sounds to me like we're gonna find some queer history!"

I look at Sterling, but I'm disturbed to see that her smile has gone from forced to wolfish.

"So!" she says. "You two are adventuring together. That's so cute. How did you guys meet, anyway?"

"Oh, well, we go to school together, but if you're asking how we became friends," Gabe says, "that happened when Ten came up to me and—"

"And asked to sit with him at lunch," I interrupt. "I'd just had a big falling-out with some friends, and Gabe had always been nice to me, so . . . I sat with him." The world does not need to know that I asked him to make out with me to make my ex jealous.

"Exactly," Gabe says without missing a beat, and I feel bad for a moment, because that's probably what he was going to say. Sterling has me feeling on edge.

"And when did you get closer?" Sterling asks.

Gabe and I look at each other, knowing what she's asking but trying to figure out the real answer. We connected almost immediately, I think. But then I left to go find some magic rings, and we were just texting, so it wasn't until I got back that we started hanging out, and it quickly became us hanging out all the time. Mostly just goofing off, joking around, talking about books and movies. He can go on about music and art in amazing ways, and he actually likes to listen to me talk about history.

"I think we just clicked right away," Gabe says, reading my mind.

"And when did you make it official?" Sterling asks, apparently unsatisfied with that dodge.

"Make what official?" I ask.

"Are you really going to keep telling me you're not a couple?" she asks. "Come on, the whole world thinks you are. That's why we're paying for Gabe to come along—a cute queer couple admiring old gay relics. People will tune in for that."

"We're just friends," I insist.

"I mean, we do bang," Gabe says, "but not, like, exclusively."

Sterling drops the camera. "Okay, no, not that."

"Not what?" I ask, amused that we've finally gotten her to stop. She starts packing the camera away.

"Look, I get it, you're going to be trouble. What fun for me," she says, not looking up. "But no one wants to think about teens—especially gay ones—having sex. That's not good for advertisers. We want you holding hands, snuggling, kissing cutely . . ." She lifts her face to meet my eyes. "Like your Instagram, your TikTok. That's the brand. You being cute with your boyfriend and talking about gay history. I can sell that. I can make you so famous."

I roll my eyes. "That's not my social media," I say.

"Wellllll . . . ," Gabe says. "It kind of is."

I frown at him.

"Not intentionally," he says quickly. "But, like—I know you want to show who you are on your socials, but it's really just this sliver of you. You use it mostly for your history videos and to take pretty photos of the city, photos of your friends—me, mostly, 'cause I'm your best-looking and best friend. And we're affectionate. To people who don't know you, we probably look like a couple, and it's not like you're posting sexy stuff, so . . ."

"Oh god," I say, realizing he might be right. How do I fix that? Show all of me?

"Exactly," Sterling says, sitting down next to me. She puts her hand on my leg, and I pull away from her. "Look, that image—that's more famous than the show right now. So we want to capitalize. Make sure there's consistency. That's going to make you famous enough that the history stuff gets out everywhere. Think of it as wrapping medicine in bacon, like for a dog."

"I'm not going to lie," I say. I shake my head, wondering why I sound like I'm negotiating with her. "I don't care about being more famous. I don't care about advertisers."

She tilts her head and looks at me. "Well, I do. And the thing is, if we lose advertisers, you lose the show."

"We can go back to the old network," I say. "We don't need—"

"Yes and no," she says. "You can. But there's a lot of legal stuff in there . . . You'd have to change the name of the show and take a break for a year because of the noncompete clause in your contract, and you wouldn't get your bonus."

I frown. "But the contract also says you can't make me do anything. I'm not going to lie. I'm not going to advertise anything."

"Your dad does," she says. She's right. We've always had sponsors. Dad turning to the camera and talking about trail mix is always so embarrassing.

"So let him do it," I say.

"You're the star now, Tenny," she says.

"Don't call me that, only my dad calls me that," I say quickly, automatically, like I have with everyone else who's tried it recently. But she's sort of right. I hadn't thought much about it, but since last season aired, all the attention has been on me. Not on Dad, like usual. I thought that was because he wasn't really on social media, and maybe it was, but my being more accessible—my posts, my videos on history— it's gotten me more followers. So maybe I am . . . not *the* star but, like, the co-star.

"Tennessee," she corrects. "Your dad told me that you're running the show. Picking the artifacts to search for, deciding who they go to. You're the boss, right? He said he's the sidekick now."

"I . . ." That is the arrangement. I kind of took over. He let me. It meant a lot at the time, but I didn't think it would come with . . .

"People don't tune in for someone's dad, even if he's kind of cute, in that old-guy way," she continues. "They tune in for the cool, young, queer archaeologist."

"Fine," I say with a sigh. I guess she's right. Which means the advertisers wanted me, not Dad, this time. "Give me some trail mix; I'll talk about how good it is."

She shakes her head but looks happy. "We've found better sponsors than that, deeper pockets. Just . . . let me handle it. You won't need to do any of those goofy to-camera moments or anything. That's what I'm here for, okay? Trust me, I'm good at my job." She puts her hand on my shoulder this time, and I don't pull back.

"Fine," I say. "But I'm not lying. I'm not saying we're a couple, or virgins, or anything."

She nods. "Okay. I can work with that. But you'll answer my questions about history?"

"Of course," I say, offended. "That's the point."

"Even if they sound silly to you, like asking if you hate Christians?"

I look out the window behind us, at the planes being ferried around the airport. In the distance, one is landing, gliding down. It looks easy. "I'll think about it," I say.

"Great," she says, standing up. "I'm going to use the ladies'. Watch my bag, okay?"

She walks off, and I slump back in my chair and turn to Gabe.

"She's something," he says.

"Yeah."

"Never had to deal with someone like her before?"

"It's like she's trying to make me politely negotiate with the people who leave nasty comments on my Instagram," I say.

He laughs. "Yeah. I mean, I get it's her job. But just ignore it. Do your thing."

"You think I can?"

"Absolutely." He hugs me tight around the shoulders and plants a kiss on my cheek. Across the aisle, an old man turns away from us. "Just focus on doing it your way. You'll be fine."

"I hope so," I say. But I can't help wondering if this is what it feels like to have who you are—your history—erased right in front of you.

❦ THREE ❦

Despite feeling anxious about Sterling, I manage to sleep on the plane with the help of some melatonin I split with Gabe. We fall asleep in the first five minutes of the movie we try to watch together. Eight hours later, Sterling shakes me awake.

"We're landing," she says. I don't know if she slept, but she seems as bright eyed and excited as before we took off. "Your dad already has a car and will meet us outside."

"Okay," I say, nudging Gabe to wake him up.

He looks up at me and blinks a few times, confused, then seems to remember everything and smiles broadly. "We here?"

"About to land," I say, feeling the plane dip down.

He stretches and rolls his neck. Something falls on the floor from the blanket we had over both our laps. I reach down to grab it—an unopened tube of bright yellow lip balm I don't recognize. THRILL is written on it in large blue letters. I show it to Gabe, but he shrugs.

"Flight attendant gave it to us?" he asks, then takes it from me and puts some on. "Nice."

He pockets it.

I feel the wheels unfurl beneath the plane and hold my breath for the initial bump as we hit the runway. When we can turn our phones on, I see I've been tagged in the official show Instagram—a photo of me and Gabe asleep on the plane, the blanket over us, the lip balm on top of that, its brand name out. Someone—Sterling, I'll bet—has captioned it: *Thrill lip balm is strong enough to protect you when you're out adventuring but still keeps your lips soft enough for special moments.*

"Ew," I say, showing it to Gabe.

He laughs aloud. "Thrill or Shill?"

I stare across the aisle at Sterling, but she won't look up.

"Can you not post stuff about me without running it by me first?" I ask her. The seat belt light goes off, and there's a symphony of clicking as everyone stands up.

"Oh come on," she says, glancing over. "You two looked so cute."

"And what's Thrill?"

"It's a makeup and skincare brand trying to move into the men's market." She opens the overhead compartment and starts wrestling out her purple wheelie bag. "I told Thrill you'd be great because you bring the gays but also can do both the sweet, kissable, young-love thing"—she finally gets the bag down and turns to us—"and the cool, adventurous, actually-takes-care-of-your-rugged-skin thing. They loved it. Perfect partnership."

I'm in the aisle, and I have to turn away from her to get my bag down from overhead, which is good, because I can feel my face turning into an arrow.

"I didn't sign anything with them," I say.

"Well, no," she says from beside me. "But you gave your dad permission to sign for advertising partnerships, and he did."

I turn around. Sterling and I are face-to-face in the aisle now. Gabe, next to me, is waiting to get out of his seat. People slowly start to file off the plane. I remember the advertising clause, going over the contract with Mom. We both assumed it was just more of Dad selling trail mix and jerky to the camera, like he'd always done. Not lip balm. And not me doing it. Nothing in the contract was about me specifically—but none of it was about Dad specifically, either. The network never mentioned my having to do anything new or different during the negotiations, either. Though they'd talked to both me and Dad like we were partners. I'd liked that. But still, I didn't think that meant I'd have to do what he had always done.

"So then take my dad's photo while he's sleeping, not mine. It's creepy. I'm seventeen."

She frowns at that. "Yeah, okay, when you say it like that, I see it. I'm sorry. I can't promise I won't take more photos of you—that's part of the job—but I'll make sure you see them before posting if it means that much to you. Okay?"

Before I can answer, the person in front of her starts moving, and she's off down the aisle, the purple wheelie bag making a gap between us as I follow.

"She sucks," Gabe says from behind me.

"I just . . . feel like she wants me to be something I'm not?"

"She does. You said you post stuff because you want people to see a full picture of you? Well she just wants people to see . . . something else, I think." He shrugs. "But at least it's just online, right?"

He's right. But still. I catch up to her when we're out in the airport.

"So, Thrill lip balm . . . Anything else I should know about?"

She smiles, genuine, like she's excited about this. "Not just lip balm. Thrill everything. They sent us sunscreen, hand cream, moisturizer. And all you have to do is use it on camera, Ten. That easy. I can make your dad do it if you really don't want to, but they want you, and they're giving us bonuses when you use the stuff on camera. And part of those bonuses go toward marketing. If we play this right, I'll have the show up for an Emmy. I'll get you on the cover of *Out*. Think of how many people you could reach that way."

Rome's airport looks like most other airports, with beige open spaces and a twisty skylight letting in the early morning light. We walk through swarms of people and their luggage. I hear Italian being spoken around me and try to remember the bits of it I know. Dad is fluent, but I know only a few phrases here and there. That's what it feels like, I realize. Like Sterling is speaking some other language, and we don't understand each other.

Being on the cover of *Out* would be great if they asked me about queer history and not my skincare, I guess, but I don't care about the Emmys. I just want to find the lyre. I don't care how moisturized my lips are while doing it. But if I don't care, why do I feel so ick?

We get to baggage claim, where Sterling has to wait for another bag. Gabe bumps me with his shoulder as we wait, and I smile.

"Adventure . . . ," he whispers.

I laugh.

"Look." He shows me his phone. He's googled Thrill Skincare and is showing me their ad campaign. "I tried googling it with 'homophobia,' too, but they're clean. Like, the lady who founded it is straight, but they use queer and trans models, give to queer charities—not anything genuinely useful, but like, lip service. And there's no record of them giving to any openly anti-queer groups or politicians, so that's a step above most companies." He shrugs. "But then again, they sell mostly in the Northeast right now. And they're not huge yet. Only just got into Sephora. So . . . like, they'll probably end up giving to some anti-queer politician eventually, and then you'll get to very publicly denounce them, right? Draw more attention to it. Win-win if you ask me."

I tilt my head. "That's true."

"You don't like it," he says.

"No," I say.

"Why?"

"I think I just hate that I have to think about it at all."

Gabe nods, then rests his head on my shoulder. "If it were me, I'd go private on everything, just do the show, never look at the comments. Think of whatever they posted as just ads . . . not you as a person."

"But other people will see those ads of me as a person."

"That's their problem, right?"

"But then it feels like . . . I'm lying somehow. Like . . ."

"Future historians?" Gabe asks.

"I know it's ridiculous to think like that."

"It isn't. It's just how you think. So maybe find a way to do it without lying? Just answer her honestly. Use the lip balm if it's good. And"—he smacks his lips—"it's not bad. Wanna taste?" He takes his shoulder away from mine and grins, leaning in for a kiss. I check that

Sterling isn't looking before kissing him on the lips, but when I pull away, she's smiling at us.

"You two are so cute," she says. She's got a new wheelie bag next to her, also purple but huge, up to her chest. "You have any bags?"

"No," I say. "Just our backpacks and duffels. I don't know where you'll have room for all that."

"It'll be fine," she says, parading toward the exit. She gets out her phone and types into it as we walk. Outside, Dad is waiting in a rented SUV. He leans out the window with a big grin, and I run up to him.

"Tenny!" he shouts. "Get in!" I open the passenger door and hop in, giving him a hug. Despite a lot of ups and downs—and there have been some very low downs—Dad and I get along pretty well now. Almost losing him made me start being more honest with him about what I needed from a father, and it turned out he wanted to give that to me . . . as long as we could keep adventuring, anyway. But I don't mind that. I kind of love that it's our thing. He wants to learn to be a good dad, and a good person, and he's willing to learn from me. And as the past months have taught me, he's genuine. He made a lot of public apologies about where relics he—well, we—recovered went to, and he did some charity work, leading tours and raising money for the peoples he should have given the relics to. I don't think it's an act, either. I think he gets it now; he still thinks what's most important is the exposure of history, not who it belongs to, but he's going to try to find a way to honor both, with me, when we can.

"Hi, Henry." Sterling is standing next to my still-open passenger door. "Good to meet you in person."

"You too," Dad says, reaching across me to shake her hand.

"I actually thought I should sit up front. It'll be better for getting shots of the road and for being able to film each of you. Ten, you sit behind your dad. Then I can pan between you and him for history and between you and Gabe for other stuff."

"'Other stuff'?" Gabe asks.

"I think it's been years since a pretty young girl asked to sit next to me," Dad says, "but sure, Ten, you and Gabe take the back seat, okay?"

"Gross." I roll my eyes and get out. "He's thinks he's flirting with her," I fake whisper to Gabe, who laughs.

"Don't be so cheesy, Henry," Gabe says, getting in the back.

"It's been a while. My moves are rusty," Dad says.

"She's a work colleague, Dad," I say with a sigh. "You shouldn't be putting moves on her anyway."

"Right." Dad nods. "Sorry."

"I saw all your previous seasons," Sterling says. "I knew what I was getting into. Which, to be clear, means you have zero chance."

I burst out laughing, and Gabe chuckles, trying to hide it.

Dad laughs, too, then turns to Gabe. "So, how are you, Gabe?"

"I am so pumped," Gabe says. "Adventure!" Clearly that's going to be his rallying cry. He squeezes my hand tightly as he says it, like he needs this for some reason. I should have asked him about it before we fell asleep on the plane.

"Adventure!" Dad shouts back, grinning. The doors are all closed now, and he drives off, away from the airport. "All right, Sterling, get that mammoth of a camera ready, and I'll tell you what I've found out and where we're going. Or"—he looks at me in the rearview—"did you give the rundown on the lyre itself yet?"

"Yeah," I say. "Apparently I hate Christians."

Dad laughs. "Me too, and I'm one of 'em." I nod. Dad is barely Christian. I remember him decorating a tree with me once, but I've never seen him in church. But I barely go to temple, and I still think of myself as Jewish because Mom and I do Hanukkah and Passover. So I guess I can't judge. He's Christian in his way.

I glance at Sterling, waiting to see if she'll pounce on Dad for a statement about his being Christian, but she's still getting her camera out. I sigh, open my bag, and take out one of the easy travel cameras I have. I turn it on.

"How about we use this?" I ask, pointing it at her. "We can always edit the footage together, so you can get, like, nice shots of Rome, and we can mix it with bumpier shots of the car."

She nods, looks almost relieved. "Yeah, yeah, let's do that, too. You can film; I can film. They wanted some higher-quality shots at the network, but it can't all be that, right?"

"Right," I say, feeling a little bad for her. This isn't all her fault, after all. The camera, the sponsorship, the questions about me hating Christianity. She works for someone else.

"Okay," I say, aiming the camera at Dad. "So, where are we going?"

Dad turns a little as he drives, smiling back at the camera. "Well, there was this dig in Jerusalem where they uncovered these ivory panels, still in pretty good condition, behind a wall in the ruins of an old temple. And these panels—they show David and Jonathan, and specifically Jonathan presenting David with a lyre. David loved to play the lyre—he was a musician before he was king—and Jonathan loved to hear him play, so there were always stories of this lyre Jonathan gave David as a testament to their friendship or love, depending on who's writing."

"Love," I say quickly.

"I think so, too," Dad says. "And the lyre's supposed to be a thing of beauty, made of ivory and decorated with gold and gems."

"Gaudy," Gabe says, and I swivel the camera to him. "I like it."

"Like a rhinestone guitar," Dad says, nodding. "Though that's not how it looked in the panel that showed Jonathan giving it to David. Looked a lot simpler there, so that part might be embellishment. Anyway, thing is, in the room where they found the panels, there was also like a pedestal—probably where the lyre went. No lyre, though. But in the room, which didn't have much else besides these broken panels, they found a Roman coin from the late eleventh century. Which is when the Crusaders sacked Jerusalem. So common sense dictates . . ."

"It was looted," I say.

"Yep," Dad says. "That's why we're in Rome. There's no record of a fancy lyre in any historical records from back then, but not a lot was recorded. It could have been taken by a soldier, a priest, or maybe it was sold, kept in a family collection, stored away somewhere. Looted antiquities are hard to find."

"So where are we starting?"

"A historical archive run by a friend of mine. For years she's kept track of anything having to do with foreign art and objects brought into Rome during the Crusades. She wants to help people hunt them down. It's at the Basilica of Saint Anthony here in Rome—that's the saint of lost objects. We gotta scour that place for any mention of anything that could be a lyre, and from there we'll see if we can figure out where to go."

"It's a treasure hunt, like, for real," Gabe says.

"Exactly," Dad says. "But you should know, we're not the only ones playing. The discovery in Jerusalem was a big press conference. A lot of people will be looking for the lyre now."

"Then we'll just have to be faster," I say.

"Let's hope," Dad says.

We're quiet for a moment, and I look out the window. It's been mostly just highway and trees, but now I can see Rome coming into view. I've been here before, but it's always stunning. Rome is one of those cities that defies modernization; silvery domes rise out of a quilt of warm orange and beige. Even from here, you can make out silhouettes and shapes that feel ancient because they are: amphitheaters, the colosseum, watchtowers. Stone pine trees crowd in the edges of the city, leaning across the border as if drawn to the beating heart of history here, the feeling of something old and weathered and filled with stories but still young and thriving and making new ones. As we drive farther in, the roads turn narrow and bumpy, and people whiz past us on mopeds. I crack open the window; it smells like pine and gasoline and that old warm smell, like hot stone, the smell of history.

The basilica Dad parks in front of is small, only a few stories high, with a domed roof and columns in front and an angled doorframe. It looks like it was probably restored at some point but long enough ago that they focused more on making it a functional building rather than a beautiful one.

It's all gray stone, even the roof, and outside there's only a small brass plaque that reads Archivi Di Viaggiatore. Under it is a bell, which Dad rings, and a moment later there's a buzz and he swings open the door, holding it for Sterling, who has brought the smaller wheelie bag with her, but left the large one in the car, at least.

Inside, the archives are much less plain. The room swoops up, filling all two stories. The walls are lined with shelves of old books and drawers. It smells the way rare-books rooms in libraries do: of decaying paper and leather, the wood of the shelves, and smoke, for some reason. There's a large chandelier hanging on a chain from the ceiling, but the room is so crowded with shelves that its light casts odd shadows. The floor is tiled in a dark ochre, like sand. Across from us, at the far end of the room, is a large desk piled high with books and papers. Behind it is a woman who stands as we enter.

She looks at Dad and for a moment seems confused but then smiles. Dad walks to her, she comes out from behind the desk, and they meet under the chandelier. She puts her hands on his shoulders and kisses him once on each cheek. Next to me, Sterling pops open her bag, now rushing to get out the camera and film this.

"Henry," she says with a heavy Italian accent. "I'm so glad to see you. But I'm surprised; I didn't think you'd have any interest in this one, with the sorts of things you've been looking for." She looks over at me and smiles, her hands falling. "And you're Tennessee, yes? *Bellissimo*, just like your father." She walks toward me and kisses me on each cheek. She's beautiful—most of Dad's contacts are beautiful women, something I try not to think too much about—and in her fifties, with long black curls and golden skin. She's wearing a purple dress that looks fashionable enough to be on a magazine cover.

"Hi," I say.

"Yeah, that's him," Dad says. "And that's his friend Gabe and our producer, Sterling. This is Mariana, an old friend."

"Are you really here about the lyre?" she asks, looking at me. "I thought you were interested in gay history."

"It is gay history," I say. "Jonathan and David were lovers."

She smiles as if amused—she clearly doesn't believe me at all. "I've heard that, yes. Well, I'll tell you what I told the others. I have no records of bejeweled lyres being looted, but many people didn't list exactly what they took—some didn't even know how to write—and many people didn't report anything to the church. So, it's up to you to see if you can find anything useful. I think it's a dead end, personally. If such a thing still existed, it would have come to light decades ago. The lyre is lost. But you are free to look."

She shrugs.

"Who else has been through here?" Dad asks.

"Oh, who you'd expect," Mariana says. "Someone from the Vatican, of course. Some young ones who gave up after half an hour. The fat one, what's his name . . . Benjamin? He gave up, too. Oh"—she smiles—"and Liat."

Dad frowns slightly. "Yeah, I saw her at the press conference. I don't know who she's working for."

I don't know the name Liat, but Dad's frown means she's competition.

"She seemed very happy when she left," Mariana says.

Dad raises his eyebrows. "Where was she looking?"

Mariana raises her hands and points with what I think is intentional slowness. "The last place she looked was at the end of that row, where there's a book on unusual musical instruments. But I should note it's from the early thirteenth century—a hundred years late."

"Still," Dad says, already walking toward where she's pointing, "a good place to start."

I wonder about the ethics of following someone else's trail rather than finding one of our own, and I'm about to say something, but Sterling speaks first.

"So, you don't believe the lyre is a queer artifact?" she asks Mariana.

Mariana shrugs. "No, I'm sorry if that offends. The Bible makes no mention of romantic love between David and Jonathan, but it does go on about David's lust for Bathsheba and the drama it caused. Also, he was married to a woman, and so was Jonathan." She shrugs elegantly. "I just think it's not there."

"Bisexuality exists," Gabe says. "And wouldn't they, like, have had to get married to women to continue their family lines?"

"Can I interview you?" Sterling asks Mariana before she can respond. "I want to get more about the history from different perspectives."

I feel my body get hot. She wants to hear different perspectives? She wants it in the show that people think it's not queer?

1. I can tell her to stop. She'll ask why, though, and I don't have a good argument there. I know how it'll go: she'll say we need to hear all sides and that if what I'm saying is true, it'll stand up to anything. And on

some level I know she's right. So why does her wanting to interview Mariana bother me so much?

2. I can just walk away, let her do this without complaint. And that feels worse, somehow.

3. I can break her camera. That's an option, right?

"Isn't the point of the show that it's Tennessee's perspective?" Gabe asks before I can decide anything. "People get straight opinions on history all the time. They loved last season because it was a queer person talking about queer history. Why would you take away the thing people like?"

I smile at him, and he smiles back. I look around for Dad to back me up, but he's already nose-deep in a book, oblivious to what's going on.

"It's absolutely going to be Tennessee's perspective," Sterling says, opening the purple bag. "We wouldn't have acquired the show if we didn't want that. But we have a bigger audience now, and we're selling to new people. It's important to make sure they see different perspectives, too. One they might relate to more."

"Why?" I ask. "They see that perspective everywhere else."

"This feels like too much drama," Mariana says, throwing up her hands. "I don't want to get involved in that. I like Tennessee; I like the show. I just don't see David and Jonathan as gay."

Sterling looks up, her camera already out of the bag. She glares at me. "It's not drama. They're just getting a little used to someone else's voice in the mix." She sighs loudly. "I promise, Ten, the show will still be your show. Mariana, please, let's just talk about this history—and this archive. I want some shots of it. Maybe you can give us a tour?"

Mariana glances over at me, but I don't know what to say to her. She doesn't believe in David and Jonathan being queer? Fine. Straight is the default for most historians. They find traditional marriage statues of two ancient Egyptian women and say, "But who knows what their relationship was?" They ignore what's staring them in the face because they can't conceive of the idea of queer people in history. Mariana can do that, too, if she wants. But I won't. And constantly arguing with Sterling is just making me lose focus.

"What do you want to do?" Gabe asks in a low voice, glancing at Sterling, who now has the camera set up and is panning over the shelves. "I can watch her, if you want to go with your dad."

I smile and feel gratitude swell up in me like the time I was in a room filled with burning oil, but . . . better. A good warm. I nod, and hand Gabe one of my small cameras. He walks over to stand next to Sterling. I don't know what he'll do, exactly, but I know he'll make sure Sterling's "both sides" viewpoint doesn't take over *my* show.

I walk down the row of shelves to Dad. He's flipping the pages of an old book, and I look over his shoulder. It looks like a ledger written in Italian but with bits of Latin I recognize. I take out my camera to film it. Someone should be filming the real history, not just pretty shots of books and differing perspectives.

"There's two entries here that I think could be the lyre," he says. "This one"—he points—"of an ancient harp covered in jewels, with an inscription in Hebrew, it says, but they wrote the entry in Italian, so they must have translated. 'Music for a king,' essentially."

"That's your English from their Italian which is from someone else's Hebrew?" I ask.

"That's biblical history, Tenny." I laugh because he's right, and he grins up at me, then spots the camera. "Shouldn't Sterling be doing that? Where is she?"

"Interviewing Mariana about why she thinks Jonathan and David weren't lovers."

"That feels like a waste of time," he says, confused. "Well, whatever, you're filming the real stuff. Let me show you the other entry." He turns back a few pages to where a note card is spacing the pages. The note card is new, not something from the library, with a lipstick kiss on it.

"What's that?" I ask.

Dad smirks. "Liat Saban. That's her shade. She probably knew I was coming. She saw me at the press conference."

"You know her lipstick shade?" I ask.

"Fire and Ice. Your mom's is Pillow Talk. Let me tell you something you will never need to know: The way to a woman's heart isn't perfume. Buy them lipstick in their favorite shade."

I sigh. "So she's, like, teasing you?"

"Yep." He grins like a dirty old man, which I guess he is. "That's Liat."

"She going to try to stop us?"

He shakes his head. "No, no, not stop us. That would ruin the fun for her. Mislead us . . . maybe. But that's more about mischief, I think. She's a good person. She was a rabbi, in fact."

"What?" I ask.

"Oh yeah. She's from LA. Her dad was a talent agent, her mom a model, but she went to rabbinical school. Was a rabbi at a Reform congregation in New York for maybe six months before she realized she hated it and what she loved was the history. Decided to go out and find it instead of preaching it. She reached out to me . . . oh, fifteen years ago? And I sort of mentored her for a few years." He grins. "She was you before you! This is all before the show, of course."

"You trained her?" I ask. "So she's probably pretty good?"

"Oh yeah. She's good. Trained by the best." He puffs his chest out proudly.

"And she's in the lead," I say, my stomach suddenly heavy with worry.

"Don't worry," Dad says. "We can catch up to Liat, and she knows it. If this"—he waves the kissed note card—"is any indication, she's hoping we'll catch up."

I frown, not just because another talented treasure hunter is after the lyre, but because of the way Dad smiles when he says it.

"Truth is," he continues, "Liat and I looked for the lyre once before, when you were a baby. We thought we had a lead in this temple outside Jerusalem. Didn't find it, though. Found some traps, and this eighth-century mezuzah that I swear would lock any door we put it next to. We had fun, but we ran out of leads on the lyre."

"So she really wants it," I say, my voice growing even more nervous.

Dad sees me and rumples my hair. "Don't worry, Tenny. But we should try to figure out who she's working for. She always needs funding—no producers nor show."

"I'm more curious about which page she marked with her . . . calling card," I say, nodding at the book.

"Yeah," Dad says. "I'm not sure if that's her trying to help us along or mislead us, or maybe it's her knowing I'll think she's misleading us and faking us out with this other entry in the book." He points. "Only other one for a harp, but it's described as very plain, and with the strings still on, which implies it was a lot younger. After a hundred years, the original strings would be gone, decayed, so these would be new ones someone put in, except they say it was found in a box of old dusty heirlooms. The fact that there were strings at all was sort of a miracle. It has an inscription, too, also in Hebrew, though translated into Latin this time, then Italian: 'For my twin.'"

"Twin?" I ask.

"It says they thought it was a gift between brothers. But there's no other harps nor lyres noted in here. Think it's the other one?"

"I guess," I say. "I mean, we're just looking at one book, following Liat, but if it's between those two, it's the king one, right? Even if David wasn't king until Jonathan died?"

"Yeah, that's what I was thinking, too. Doesn't seem quite right. Liat is good, but everyone makes mistakes. Or, again, she could be trying to fake us out . . . but honestly, I don't think she'd do that here. She's mischievous, but she likes the idea of beating people fair and square. And she'd never steal a book or anything—at least not from Mariana."

"So you think this king lyre is the best choice?" I ask.

"We could look around some more," he says. "Maybe she's wrong and we'll find a real lead."

"Where is the king lyre?"

"Says it was displayed in a wealthy merchant family's home in Venice. They claimed it was bought off a Crusader."

"Venice, okay." I nod. "And where's the twin harp? What's it say?"

"Also Venice. It was bought by a church in Venice: Santa Cecilia. The seller says he found it in the attic. It was just . . . brought back from the Crusades and passed down through generations in the attic like that. Amazing."

"History gets forgotten, right?" I say. "So much queer history comes from, like, letters people find hidden in their attics."

"Straight history, too," Dad says. "History is made of whatever survives, right?"

"Yeah. But I guess if it's not the king one, we can check out the twin one."

"Yeah . . . ," he says, scanning the other shelves.

"Should we look around a little more?" I ask. "Just make sure we didn't miss anything?"

He taps his foot, staring at the book. "We can always come back if we need to, but in a race—and that's what this is feeling like now—you need to be decisive, fast. I say we check out this king lyre in Venice."

"Okay," I say. "I trust your instincts. So . . . Venice."

"Let's go," Dad says, shooting photos of both entries in the book on his phone before putting it back. We walk back down the aisle to the room's center, where Sterling finally has the camera set up and is filming Mariana behind her desk.

"Gay history exists, of course," Mariana is saying, "but it's very difficult to prove. And proof is what makes history."

"You can't prove David loved Bathsheba," I say.

She glances up at me and raises an eyebrow. Sterling keeps the camera on Mariana, but Gabe points the small camera I gave him at me.

"What?" Mariana asks.

"You're saying that because the story of Bathsheba is explicitly about David's love for her and is in the Bible, it's real. But the Bible has been translated a hundred times over—no one has the original. The words themselves have changed. The word *homosexual* didn't even appear in it until the 1950s. *Sodomite* wasn't a word until the 1600s. Before then, people understood the sins of Sodom were rape, and that Leviticus said not to lie with male pagan temple prostitutes. But things get changed and translated . . ." I trail off as an idea hits me. "It's the twin harp," I say, turning to Dad. "There's a phrase David and Jonathan called each other in Hebrew. I found it a few times in my research: *nephesh teomim*. It means, like, 'soulmate,' but it gets translated different ways, like 'kindred spirit' or sometimes 'twin spirit.'"

"'For my soulmate,'" Dad says, smiling. "Yeah, that works better than 'king.'"

"Okay," I say, "so let's go."

"Did we figure it out already?" Sterling asks, looking worried. "I thought I'd have time to film—"

"Sterling, we're in a race. We gotta get moving," Dad says. "I'm sorry, but I told you this is how it would be."

She sighs. "You did. I thought you were exaggerating, but . . ." She starts packing up her camera, quickly this time. "Thanks for talking to me," she says to Mariana as we wait by the door.

"She say anything awful?" I ask Gabe.

"Didn't really have time," Gabe says. "Plus I kept accidentally getting in the shot. Silly me."

I laugh and reach out to squeeze his hand.

"You found something for a soulmate?" he asks.

"A harp," I say. "Not decorated, like, on the ivory, but . . . I think it's right. Maybe. We'll see. And now we go to Venice."

Gabe laughs. "I barely got to see Rome."

❧ FOUR ❧

Rome to Venice is just as fast by train as by plane, and Sterling says it'll give her a chance to get B-roll of the countryside, so she gets us tickets on the high-speed train. We haven't even unpacked, and we're leaving Rome already. I feel sort of sad about that, but excited that we're on the trail of the lyre. There's something about being on the hunt for an artifact. Mom says Dad always acted like an addict when he was chasing one, and . . . she's not so wrong. The truth is, I get it. There's this feeling of something being so close, and if you just figure out one more thing, go to one more city, you'll get it. And the reward is worth it—getting to show off that history and, by doing that, getting to be part of it. I mean, I know my queer history is mine no matter what, but there's a difference. Right now, I'm standing in Rome, one of the oldest cities in the world, feeling the air around me and knowing someone stood here feeling the air around them more than a thousand years ago. A thousand! That makes me feel part of something. Finding a relic is like that but times a million. You get proof that you're part of something special.

"I'm sad we're leaving so soon," Gabe says, standing next to me in front of the train station. Dad and Sterling are returning the rental car. "But it's kind of fun to already be going on to the next thing. I wish I'd watched you figure out the clue, though."

"You did! Until I was correcting Mariana, I thought it was the other lyre."

"I guess, I mean, I wish I was . . . doing more? Like, I wanted to come to do all the stuff Leo did, jumping into traps and stuff."

I laugh. "He also just watched me and my dad pore over books for hours to translate stuff. We cut that part, though. Not good TV."

"Tennessee Russo," says a voice behind me. I turn around and find myself closer than I'd like to be to a man in a leather jacket and jeans. Actually, he's pretty cute for an older guy, maybe forties, with pale skin and thick black hair with a white streak through it. Then I spot what he's wearing under the leather jacket: a priest's collar.

"That's me," I say, glancing at Gabe and looking around for my dad.

"It's lovely to meet you," he says. He has a faint accent. Dutch, maybe? Norwegian? "I'm Father Eriksen, from the Vatican." He smiles, and I get the impression of a teacher about to scold a student and enjoy it. "I was hoping we could speak."

"Sure," I say. "What about?"

"The lyre," he says slowly, his hands lifting, like he's trying to calm an angry dog. "The Vatican is concerned that your pursuit of it indicates you'll be twisting biblical history to fit the narrative your show aims to create. We'd prefer it if you pursued something else. The lyre is a Catholic artifact. It belongs with us. Not lied about on television." The words come out politely, professionally, which makes it all the worse. Like we're in on something, and we both know I'm lying. I can feel rage jolt through my body like lightning.

"I wasn't planning on lying." I try to keep my tone even, but the anger makes it hard.

He stares at me for a moment, as if trying to translate me. "I see. But you are pursuing the lyre?"

"Yes," I say carefully. Behind me, Gabe coughs nervously.

"And you believe that it is somehow related to your . . . homosexuality?"

"Not mine, exactly. But I believe Jonathan and David were in love."

"Not all love is base, Tennessee," he says, smiling softly.

Gabe coughs again and taps me on the shoulder. I look at him, and he nods, motioning a few feet behind Father Eriksen. Two large men stand in black suits and sunglasses, watching us.

"Don't mind them," Father Eriksen says. "They're just my helpers."

"So this isn't a shakedown?" I ask.

He looks confused for a moment, then shakes his head. "Shakedown. Threat? No. On the contrary, the Vatican would be so pleased if you ended your pursuit of the lyre and promised never to mention it on your television show. So pleased, in fact, that we would be willing to demonstrate that gratitude financially."

"So it's a payoff?" I ask, feeling a warm flush of pride—I'm important enough to pay off!—before remembering what he's paying me off to do.

"It is an offer of a gift to express our appreciation of your understanding . . . if you understand?"

I smile as wide as I can, trying to match his professional tone. "I do understand."

"Wonderful," he says.

"Ten?" I hear Dad's voice behind me, worried. He steps closer, and I can hear Sterling's wheelie bag on the stones following him.

"I understand, and I refuse," I say. "We're going to find the lyre, we're going to put it on the show, and we're going to tour with it and talk all about how Jonathan and David loved each other. Romantically. Physically. Basely."

Father Eriksen's eyes flicker down for a moment, and he looks disappointed, the way a parent would be. "I see. Well, then I imagine we'll meet again. But I urge you to reconsider. The offer remains open for a while. The Vatican wants to cooperate, Tennessee."

"The Vatican?" I hear Sterling choke as she repeats it.

Father Eriksen looks up at Dad. "Perhaps your father will understand, after you discuss it. Have a lovely trip to Venice." He nods at each of us one by one, the fact that he knows where we're going hitting me like a sharp slap. Then he walks away, the two men in suits following him.

"The Vatican?" Dad asks, thrilled. He claps me on the back. "You stared down the Vatican, Tenny. Nice work."

I smile at him and suddenly feel a little wobbly. The Vatican is powerful. Really powerful. And I just did that—without even thinking about it, without even making a list. But I couldn't give up on the lyre. I knew that. Still. Laughter bubbles out of me, ridiculous, a stress laugh.

Gabe laughs, too. "That was terrifying," he says.

"What did they want?" Sterling asks, her voice shrill.

"To pay us to stop looking for the lyre," I say.

She stares at me silently for a full ten seconds, blinking. "And you said no?"

"Yeah," I say, as though it's the most obvious thing in the world. She looks at me for a long time before flicking her eyes to Dad.

"Henry, let's get on the train. I think you and I should talk alone."

Dad laughs. "Sure, Sterling. Let's get on the train." He looks at me and winks, and I smile. He's got my back in this.

The train is waiting in the station, so we get on and find our seats, the four of us grabbing two tables across the aisle from each other. The train is sleek and modern, high speed, with white tables and walls and big windows. Everything gleams. I sit next to Gabe at one table, across the aisle from Dad, who sits across from Sterling. Sterling starts to take out her camera, cleaning the lenses, her whole body radiating annoyance.

We're all quiet until Gabe says, "So where are we going in Venice?"

"Santa Cecilia," I say.

"And the lyre is there?" Gabe asks, sounding disappointed.

I laugh. "Maybe? I think probably not, though. They'd know if they had something important, I think . . . I mean, I guess it could just be in storage. But they could have sold it, too. It's been, like, eight hundred years. Who knows? But it's the next place to go, where the trail leads." I smile at him and realize he's been filming me.

"And we need to look out for Liat," Dad says. "She's looking, too, and she knows me."

"And the Vatican," Gabe adds.

Sterling huffs.

The train starts to move, and we're all quiet, watching the station turn into a tunnel and then into the city blazing past, all that history whizzing by in seconds in a watercolor splash of orange, yellow, green, and blue.

"Bye, Rome," Gabe says, waving out the window adorably. I put my arms around his waist and squeeze, laying my head on his shoulder and watching the scenery.

"We can come back sometime," I tell him. "Really see it. But now, adventure, right?"

"Adventure!" He points in the direction the train is moving.

"Henry," Sterling says, her voice so calm it's clearly fake. Her camera is back in its case now, her hands folded in her lap. "I think we should talk. Alone."

Dad laughs. "You know I'm just going to tell everything to Tenny anyway. We make the decisions together."

I don't look across the aisle at Dad, but I watch him in the reflection of the window. He's watching me, and I can feel his trust, his pride in me, and I feel . . . armored. Like I can handle Sterling and her weird arguments and advertising, even if I don't understand why it upsets me. I take out my phone and grab a selfie of me and Gabe, with Gabe sticking out his tongue, and then take a photo of our view. I post them both on Instagram. I'm smiling really broadly.

This whole time, Sterling has been quiet, formulating what she wants to say. Finally, she clears her throat.

"We should consider the Vatican's offer," she says finally.

Dad laughs. "No, Sterling."

"Henry!" Her hands go up and slam back down on the table. She sounds surprised. Clearly she doesn't know Dad. "They're offering money. That means more advertising, marketing going right into the show. We just switch our focus back to Wilde's tomb. It's a win-win." Her hands fly up again, small explosions of fingers.

"Sterling, we choose the artifacts to pursue," Dad says. "Not you, and not the Vatican."

"Consider what they can do if they don't like the . . . angle of the show, though? Denounce it publicly? Imagine what happens then. More than twenty percent of Americans are Catholic. And you have a big international following." Now the hands have clasped together, elbows on the table, almost in prayer.

"Yeah," Dad says, leaning back, folding his arms. "Think of the free publicity that would bring."

She's quiet for a moment. "True," she says. "But think of our sponsors. I don't know if Thrill would want to be involved with a show condemned by the pope. Maybe . . ." She takes out her phone. "Okay, the founder isn't Catholic, but still. Employees, consumers . . ."

"Then they drop us," Dad says with a shrug. "We have a contract with them for this season, right? I saw the clauses that say they understand the show has a particular viewpoint. I believe that viewpoint is what they liked, right?"

"Henry . . . it would be so easy to take the deal. Please, consider it." The hands are still now. She's just staring at him.

Dad shakes his head. "It ain't happening. But I tell you what: I'll put on some of that Thrill sunscreen right now, do one of those talks to the camera about how it feels so nice on my skin."

Now Sterling laughs. "That's not how we do things anymore, but . . ." She looks over at me. "Ten, why don't you and Gabe put some on? I can film it."

"Not me?" Dad asks.

"Yeah, use Dad," I say.

"They want your youth and relationship," Sterling says, turning to me completely, legs in the aisle. "Please? You owe me if we're not going to take the Vatican's deal."

"I . . ." I shake my head. I'm so tired of fighting with her. It's taking all the fun out of this. "Fine."

"He doesn't owe you," Gabe says. "This is the show you signed on for. Him not changing it for you doesn't mean he owes you."

Sterling frowns. "But I'll be able to show Thrill what they're paying for when I warn them about the . . . content. You need sunscreen, anyway. It'll be so easy." Suddenly her eyes light up. "Oh! Maybe you can put it on each other? Like, you can dab a little on Gabe's nose?"

"Absolutely not," I say. "But fine, you can film me putting some on."

Gabe raises his eyebrow at that. Maybe I'm compromising too much, but I do want to get this season out there more, this history out there more. So maybe that takes a little compromise.

"Fantastic," she says. "See? I knew we could all work something out . . ." She opens her purse and takes out a tube of Thrill sunscreen, which she puts on the table. "I still think we should take the Vatican's deal—we could do a great season on Wilde and less controversial, just, like, happy, gay, love-is-love history, right?"

"I'm putting on the sunscreen," I say. "Don't push your luck."

"Fine," she says, sounding cheerful, and turns the camera on me. I sigh and take the tube of sunscreen. "Look happy about it, please," she says.

I force a smile and rub some sunscreen onto my arms and neck, trying to look natural.

"You want?" I ask Gabe.

He goes to take it from me, his face wearing a smile so fake that I start laughing, and my hands, slippery with the lotion, let the tube slip up into the air, where I grab for it, but it slips again, and Gabe grabs it out of the air, both of us laughing.

"Oh, that was good," Sterling says. "Thrill will love that." Gabe and I both stop laughing. Gabe sighs and puts the lotion on his arms in silence.

"Let's go get something to eat," I say to Gabe. I turn to Dad. "Want anything?"

"Muffin or something, sure," Dad says.

"Coke Zero," Sterling says.

I clamber up from the seat, and Gabe follows me down the aisle toward the cafeteria car. Outside the train, the scenery has turned to fields of some kind of crop—wheat? Nothing ripe, just tall green fronds, a blur as we go by them.

"I can't believe she wanted me to take the deal," I say.

"I'm not," Gabe says. "I'm just shocked she thought anyone would say yes."

"She's the worst."

"Capitalism." He shrugs. "No ethical consumption, right? You're being consumed."

I laugh. "I don't think so . . . unless you have plans for tonight."

He grins. "Oh, for sure I have plans. But you know what I mean. You're the product now." We walk into the cafeteria car, our bodies swaying in the little passway between cars. It smells like coffee, which normally I can't stand but smells good here. Maybe because I'm hungry, or maybe because it's Italian. Of course, there's a line.

"The history is the product," I say, taking my place in line behind a thin woman in a sundress.

He nods. "It *should be* the product. But not with Sterling. She's selling you. History, sure, archaeology, adventures, but you're the show to her. She thinks you're what's selling everything."

I shake my head. "But I'm not. It's the history."

Gabe kisses me on the mouth. "I love you so much that you think that."

"What?"

"Dude, last season was about history, sure, but it was about more—it was watching this hot gay teenager reunite with his dad, figure out history, meet a cute boy after a breakup . . . People watched for you, for your story. And the history was a part of that, but it wasn't like . . . a documentary. Most people didn't watch to learn. I mean, they totally did, but they didn't watch *for* that. They watched for drama. Which you're at the center of."

"I . . ." I frown. "But it's about the history."

"To you. Not to the people watching you. Why do you think you got so many followers? And Sterling is trying to make money off that—for the show. I mean, she's not wrong that the more you put of yourself out there, the more you can get back to promote yourself. You just have to figure out where your line is."

"I . . . I don't think I mind just being me and people seeing that," I say. "But I feel like she's making me . . . something else?"

"A product," Gabe says. "That's what I'm saying."

I stare at the counter ahead of us, where little food items are displayed under a glass counter, like at the movies. Brightly wrapped Italian candy bars I don't recognize. Soda bottles and cans. Am I one of those?

"How do you know so much about this?" I ask him.

"My parents. The art world is like this, too. Smaller scale, but . . . kinda cutthroat. You should talk to your dad about it. I mean, he did it all the previous seasons, right? The product placement? And he cares about the history. So maybe his line will help you find yours."

"Yeah," I say. "That's a good idea."

"But here, give me your phone."

I take out my phone and hand it to him. He pulls up Instagram and finds a photo I took from the tour with the rings. It's a photo of the rings on their pedestal and my reflection in the glass case around them. I captioned it: *It's amazing to see myself in history that gets its own exhibit.*

"Cringe," I say.

Gabe laughs, then scrolls to the comments.

"No, don't do that!" I say loudly enough that the person in front of us in line looks back.

Gabe ignores me, still scrolling. He finds a recent comment, only a few weeks old: "I watched the whole season and tried to tell my history teacher about it, but he said that sexuality in ancient Greece was different and the idea of queer didn't exist. He won't even let me do a project on the rings."

I frown. "Why are you showing me this?" I ask.

"Respond," Gabe says.

"Respond? You told me never to read them."

"I did. But now we're trying something different. Sterling wants to make you the product? You fight back by being all about the history— by being whatever version of you that you want to show the world. The parts you love. I'm trying to make you love this, too."

"Do I seem like I don't love it?"

"The marketing stuff is definitely getting in your head."

I laugh. "Yeah . . . okay." I take the phone and respond to the comment:

"Well, first of all, 'ancient Greece' is a vague term. It covers hundreds of years and a huge area, so we can't say that all ancient Greeks felt exactly the same way about sexuality everywhere the whole time. But your teacher is sort of right—the ancient Greeks didn't have an idea of queerness that lines up with ours. To them, sex was about who was penetrating and who got penetrated. Often, a younger man would partner with an older guy, working as a sort of intern to learn about the older guy's profession and also . . .

have sex with them. But not all the time—because not every man wanted to have sex with men. And then, of course, there were men who much preferred it and even liked being on the penetrating end when they were older—which was scandalous behavior. But even if our definitions and how we view sex aren't the same, it doesn't cancel out that there were men who pursued and enjoyed having sex with men—and the same with women. And those people, by today's standards, would be queer. They're our ancestors. The Sacred Band was made up of men like that. So just because they didn't experience the same sort of prejudice or define themselves quite the same, that doesn't make it not gay. Before Christianity took over through colonization, everywhere all over the world had so many different ideas about sex and gender. Many cultures had more than two genders. Same-sex desire was often viewed differently. That doesn't mean those people aren't queer. If anything, it proves that queerness has always been here, and that it's only homophobia that erases us. So I say do that project anyway, and tell your history teacher that while the ancient Greeks may not have thought of themselves as gay or straight, the act of same-sex desire was still there and is still worth doing a project on. Good luck!"

I finish typing, and we're at the cafeteria counter.

"Feel better?" Gabe asks.

"So much," I say, squeezing his hand. I do. I feel a million times lighter, like I could float out the window. "Thanks. You're right. I let it get in my head so much that I forgot why I love doing this."

We order, getting sandwiches for ourselves, and a cornetto and Coke Zero for Dad and Sterling, before heading back to our seats.

"So," I say, "you just helped me out a lot . . . and I feel like I've been neglecting you."

"Neglecting?" Gabe asks.

"Why did you want to come?" I ask.

"Adventure!" he responds quickly with a big grin.

"I know, but . . . why?"

He sighs a little, then catches himself on the wall as the train shakes. "This is going to sound ridiculous. And, like . . . vain, I guess?"

"Vain?"

"So . . . in the fall, I'll be applying early to Oberlin. Double degree, both the college and the conservatory. Everyone seems to think it's a sure thing . . . and then I guess I'll do five years there, get a master's degree in composition, maybe go to Eastman . . . and I'll write symphonies and music and . . ." He shakes his head. "It's all just so laid out for me."

"Laid out?" I ask, opening the door to the next compartment.

"My life. It's . . . planned. I can see it all stretching ahead of me, like a road, and it's a nice road! I feel terrible complaining. I like the life I see ahead of me . . . but it's also just . . . there."

"That's bad?" I ask, confused. I stop walking down the aisle to look at him. His brow is furrowed. "You can be as vain as you want with me, you know. I just want to understand."

"Your life is so cool," he says. "I mean . . . you're cool." The train sways as we look at each other.

"So are you," I say, leaning against him since I can't take his hand, as we're both holding food.

"Yeah, but you don't know what's around the corner. Your life isn't a road. It's twisty and exciting and . . ."

"Adventure-filled?"

"Yeah." He smiles, a little sad. Behind him, someone else is trying to get down the aisle, so we start moving again. "And it's nothing to complain about. Like I said, the life I have is great. I can't wait to write symphonies for orchestras, maybe an opera . . . but it feels like . . ."

"You don't have any adventure left?"

"I know, I know. I'm seventeen; I have my whole life ahead of me, filled with adventure. It sounds ridiculous."

I touch my forehead to his, then lean back. "It doesn't. I'm going to school for archaeology—I don't know where yet, that's true. And then I'll . . . get a PhD in it probably, go on digs, teach . . . but that's not what I think about when I think about the future. I think about the show, about . . . these adventures. So I get it."

"I don't sound vain?"

"I mean, sure thing to get into Oberlin, maybe," I say with a laugh. "But it's true, too. So no."

He laughs. "And you get why I want adventure?"

"Same reason I do," I say. "I think sometimes life starts to look all . . . prepared. But it's fun to be unprepared, too."

"That's what I want. Unprepared adventure."

"Well . . ." I laugh and start walking again. "You're getting it. We saw Rome for like five minutes."

"True. But I feel bad I missed you guys going through the books or whatever. I know you said it was boring, but it's part of the adventure, right?"

"Oh," I say. "I'm sorry."

"I mean, I offered to watch Sterling and Mariana. I guess I just didn't realize it would be so fast."

"No, absolutely. Stick with me . . . Sterling will . . . do what she does. I think I'm just going to try to be boring, if that makes sense. No more giggling as the sunscreen slips from my hands."

"Oh yeah, that footage will make her week."

"I'm just going to talk about the history and do my thing, like you said."

"And if she wants to get a 'differing view'?"

"Then I'll ignore it. She wants drama? Well, let's give her nothing."

"Oh yes," Gabe says. "Giving nothing! I love it. But . . . we can also try to disrupt a little."

"Disrupt?"

He wiggles his eyebrows. "Yeah. If you want. Just . . . trust me. Let me do my thing. I think that'll be more adventure for me. Gotta improv. Unprepared chaos."

"Chaos?" He wiggles his eyebrows again, and I laugh. "Okay, do your thing."

We get back to our seats, and I hand Dad a cornetto and Sterling her Coke Zero. Her camera is fixed on the scenery outside, at least, and not me.

"Thanks," Dad says. "You okay?"

"Yeah," I say. "I'm just getting used to being the star, I think." I glance over at Sterling. She smiles at me like I've apologized for something.

"Co-star," Dad says. "I mean, some people must still watch for me, right?"

"Sure, Dad," I say. "Old people."

Dad laughs. "Yeah, ancient historians peering at the screen through their three-inch-thick glasses. Decrepit, ancient, maybe in their"—he pauses dramatically—"fifties."

"Do people live that long?" Gabe asks.

Sterling gets up and shuffles off to the bathroom, which is great, because now I can really ask Dad for advice.

"Dad, how did you do ads?"

"How?" He looks confused. "Well, I just turned to the camera and—"

"No," I interrupt. "Not literally how. I mean, how did you do them and not feel gross about it?"

"Gross?" He raises an eyebrow. "I mean, they were cheesy, but it was just selling jerky and trail mix. Batteries that one time."

"Yeah, but . . ." I sigh and look over at Gabe, who nods slightly, telling me to go on. But I don't know what I'm asking.

"Tenny?" Dad looks worried now. I get up and go sit across from him. Gabe nods, like he's going to stay out of this one, and turns to look out the window.

"I just . . . all the stuff Sterling is asking me to do. It feels gross, somehow. Like I'm not me."

"Oh . . . well, when you're selling something, you're not. You're a salesman. But I don't think anyone looks at those moments when I'm talking about trail mix and thinks, 'Yeah, that's Henry's whole personality.'"

"But they think it's a part of it," I say. "Someone probably refers to you as the jerky guy."

Dad laughs so hard, he slaps his leg. "Maybe," he says after a moment. "Never thought of that. That's pretty funny, though."

"Okay, but imagine it wasn't 'the jerky guy,' but it was, like . . ." I shake my head. It's not the product. I don't care about sunscreen and lip balm. "Okay, so on social media, people are always assuming things about me and saying things, right?"

"Like the homophobes?"

I shake my head. "They suck, but I can block them. It's more people saying stuff like 'you're so cute' and 'yay love is love' and stuff."

"But those are good. I mean, love is love, right? That's the gay motto. And you take after me, so you're a good-looking guy."

"But they're ignoring what I'm talking about. I want to teach them about queer history, not just . . . be a token gay teen they can feel good about supporting."

Dad furrows his brow and blows out a deep breath. "I mean, they're watching, though, right? I'm sorry, Tenny, I'm not really seeing the problem."

"I just want people to see me as . . . me. Not just some cute gay boy selling lip balm. I'm a historian. I'm . . . more than all that."

"Well sure, but this is TV. They're not sitting down to get to know you. They're watching you explore history. And if they tune in because you've got my cheekbones"—he winks—"then you're just carrying on a tradition. Plenty of ladies tuned in to the first season because they thought I was cute. Maybe men, too," he says, as if just realizing that's a possibility.

I sigh. I feel like he doesn't get what I'm saying. But I'm not even sure what I'm saying, so I can't blame him.

He squeezes my shoulder and looks me in the eye. "Look, Tenny, this isn't real life. TV, social media . . . people might tune in because we're cute or because they want to support gay teens, but so what? They're still tuning in. So sell the lip balm! What does it cost you, except maybe being a little cheesy? Think they're going to make a GIF of it?"

I hadn't considered that. I feel my blood rush from my head and drain out of my body until I'm just an empty vessel waiting to be filled with potential humiliation.

Dad laughs at the face I'm making. "Don't worry, you can do multiple takes. Sterling will make sure it's not GIF-worthy."

I take a breath. At least there's that. Still, it feels wrong.

"Look," Dad says. "When we look at history, historical people, we know we're just assembling something out of pieces we find, right? Here's something he wrote, or something written about her, but we don't know a full picture. We need to fill in the blanks. That's what people do when they see folks on TV."

"But what if they fill them in wrong?"

Dad shrugs. "That's their problem. The truth comes out eventually. And even if it doesn't—you know who you are. Who cares if people misinterpret you?"

I'm quiet at that. I look at my feet. Why *do* I care? "Because I'm queer," I say finally. "And queer people are always misinterpreted. I mean, I don't think anyone is going to say I'm straight, but . . . saying I'm just this adorable symbol, a rainbow emoji, the human version of the phrase 'love is love'—isn't that erasing queerness, too?"

Dad considers that for a moment, scratching at his stubble. "I . . . don't know, Tenny. I'm sorry. I don't know what it's like to be a young gay man . . . but I'm sorry if my saying 'love is love' is . . . bad?"

"No." I sigh. "It's not bad. I didn't mean that. I just mean . . . I don't want to be *just* that. I don't want any queer person to be *just* that. Like, that's fine, but it's not the same as seeing me as a person. Or being genuinely supportive. Tweeting 'love is love' isn't the same as, like, protesting the new queer book bans or the terrible anti-trans laws that politicians are passing. Buying lip balm because I'm selling it isn't supporting queer people."

"Well, yeah," Dad says. "But do you think people really believe it is?"

"It feels that way sometimes."

"Well, maybe you can talk about that on camera, then?" Dad says. "Ask Sterling. I bet she'd be into it."

"Yeah," I say. But I still feel confused. I still can't say exactly why I hate the idea of doing these ads.

"Now we gotta get to work," Dad says, glancing up. Sterling is coming back down the aisle. "So, this church—we should try to find out about it."

"Right," I say, going back to my seat across from Gabe and taking out my tablet. "Research time. You wanted to watch, right, Gabe? Well, here comes the exciting part."

❧ FIVE ❧

A few hours later, as we pull into Venice, we don't know much more about Santa Cecilia. It has a Wikipedia page, but it's short. It was built sometime in the 1180s and has been destroyed and rebuilt a bunch of times since then. Which means if the church had the lyre, it could have been lost in a fire or a flood. I try not to focus on that, though. It's a small church, northeast of the Rialto Bridge, tucked away between a piazza and a much larger church, and accessible only by a narrow alley along one of the canals. It's operated by a convent, with some people visiting to pray—musicians mostly—and a few musical recitals on special days.

"We should go to the hotel first," Dad says. "We can't drive around Venice, we can't carry all this stuff, and it's already two in the afternoon, so I think we'll be staying the night here. Sterling, you can book us some rooms, right? Three okay, or do you want a separate room, Gabe?"

Gabe looks at me, and I nod that I'm good with sharing. I sort of assumed we would.

"Three is fine, thank you," Gabe says.

Dad nods and doesn't say anything, which I'm grateful for. He and Mom used to tease me or give me safe-sex talks whenever I was sharing a room with a boy, but the past few months, seeing more of Gabe, they've relaxed, I think. They know him, so they're more chill about the idea of us sharing a bed. Though a hotel is sort of different, I guess. I wonder if it'll feel different.

Sterling gets on the phone. She's good at this part of her job, at least, because by the time the train stops, we have rooms at the Hotel Melodia, which is a short walk from Santa Cecilia.

Venice isn't like Rome, with its wide horizon and golden stone. Venice is crowded, people huddling together on a too-small island as the sea rises. It smells like the water—that brackish mix of salt and fresh—and like fish, but also of warm glass and flowers. Light cuts through the buildings like knives, so bright the shadows seem diluted. More than all that, though, it's a maze. Bridges, alleys, streets that ram into small, magical, dead-end courtyards with views of the water. Others that wind into marketplaces alive with color and shouting. Turn a corner; you're somewhere new. Turn back, and where you came from is gone.

"This is amazing," Gabe says, taking it all in. "I hope we get to see at least a little of it."

"We'll take a boat to the hotel," Dad says. "You can see a lot that way."

We grab our things, and Dad hires a motorboat to take us around the north side of the city, under the bridge our train just rolled over. I've been here before, so I film Gabe smiling as he watches the way the edge of the city seems to just fall into the water and the brightly colored houses and the vines that trail off their balconies, wrapping the outside of the city in a blanket.

"This is amazing," he says. "How is this real?"

"Lagoons provided protection from mainland armies," Dad says. "Though now, of course, with climate change . . . it floods a lot. They put raised wooden platforms over the streets, and they have a plan to help shore everything up, but then the water gets really low sometimes, too, from drought . . ."

No one says anything back. Gabe points at an old building with narrow windows and a carved front door that opens right onto the water. "So cool," he says.

"Maybe you could put on some of the lip balm?" Sterling asks me. "It's windy. You don't want chapped lips."

"Oh wait, I got this," Gabe says, taking out his stick of lip balm. "Just say something nice about it, and use it, right?"

"Yes!" Sterling says, excited. She points the camera at Gabe, who takes off the cap and starts twisting out the lip balm . . . and keeps twisting and twisting until almost the whole thing is out. Then he plucks the waxy stick out of its plastic case, pops it in his mouth, and smiles.

"Thrill tastes delicious," he says to the camera.

I burst out laughing, and Sterling sighs.

"I guess we'll find out for sure how nontoxic it is soon," Gabe adds. Sterling drops the camera and turns away.

"I'm just trying to help," she says, her voice barely audible. "Money is publicity. Publicity is power to tell your story. I just want to help you do that." She looks sad and turns away, back to filming the city. I sigh, suddenly feeling bad for her.

The boat turns down a canal and drops us off at a dock next to our hotel. We check in but just ask the porters to take our stuff to our rooms, and then we head out again. It's getting late, and we want to get to Santa Cecilia before it closes. Venice is hard to navigate, even with a map, and when we finally find the alley to turn down, I'm half convinced it can't be right. It winds around the back of a building and leads to a small courtyard with a tree. Behind the courtyard is a squat, ancient-looking building with a carved image of Saint Cecilia over the doors, her head down, playing a viola. She seems completely uninterested in us.

Sterling films the building before focusing on us. Dad is about to pull open one of the heavy wooden doors, but they start opening on their own. He backs up to avoid getting hit. A woman strides out, spots him, and breaks into a huge grin.

"Henry," she says, leaning forward, her arms around his waist for a moment as she kisses him on the cheek. It leaves a red lipstick mark.

"Liat," he says, his voice amused. They look at each other in silence for a moment, and I feel like there's a thousand things between them, but I have no idea what they are. Something tells me I don't want to know.

"I knew I should have taken the train instead of flying." Liat sighs. "We were held up in the air and circled for half an hour, and then spent another half hour of waiting on the runway." She shrugs. "Well, I guess it's more fun this way."

I take a minute to study her. She's in her forties, thin, and dressed sensibly, in sturdy hiking books, jeans, and a leather jacket over a white tee, like Dad. Her skin is dark bronze and her black hair is short, like Audrey Hepburn's but messier. She puts her hand on her hip and studies me like I'm studying her.

"So you're Tennessee. I've seen you on the show, of course, but you really do look like your dad." She winks. "Handsome, I mean. And you're smart. This'll be lots of fun."

I glance at Sterling, who is filming, a look of glee on her face.

"Who are you working for, Liat?" Dad asks.

"Why? Who are you working for?"

"The Vatican?"

She bursts out laughing. "God, no, never. I'm working for the USJHA—United States Jewish Historians Association. They have funding from a variety of Jewish museums, and when I retrieve the lyre, it'll go on tour to every one of them, in constant rotation, sharing some important Jewish history."

"And queer history," I say.

"It is." She nods at me. "I agree with you on that. But I don't get involved in how they curate it."

I smile a little. After Mariana, it's nice to hear someone agree that David and Jonathan were queer without my having to convince them. "And who are these? Boyfriend? Girlfriend?"

Sterling huffs. "I'm the producer," she says, camera raised to Dad and Liat. "Just pretend the camera isn't here."

"And I'm his best friend, Gabe," Gabe says, grinning. I can tell he thinks Liat's cool. And if I'm being honest, so do I. "Nice to meet you."

"You too. And I'm happy to sign any release forms you need," Liat says to Sterling. "The world shouldn't miss out on all this." She poses, gesturing at her face. "Just don't ask me to talk to the camera. Now, where are you staying?" She takes a wallet from her coat pocket, and it takes both Dad and me a moment to realize it's his.

"Liat," he says flatly.

She pulls his hotel room key card out of the wallet. "The Melodia? Me too. Maybe we can all do dinner together . . . , if you figure out what's in there in time."

"What's in there?" I ask, narrowing my eyes.

"You'll see. And don't worry; I put everything back exactly as I found it. Careful of the poison needles, though."

She winks, then puts his key card back in his wallet. She pauses for a moment, considering, then takes a ten-euro note from the wallet and pockets it. "I believe you owe me a drink," she says before tossing the wallet back to Dad. "I'll be in the hotel bar, after I take a shower." She grins and runs her hands through her hair, then leans forward and kisses Dad, on the other cheek this time, leaving another mark. With both lipstick smudges, it's almost like he's wearing blush. I'd say she's performing for the camera, but she hasn't even glanced at it once. I think this is all for Dad.

"Later, Henry. Nice meeting all of you." She waves, then jogs away, turning around once at the twist in the alley to shoot finger guns at us before vanishing.

"She's fun," Gabe says after a moment.

"She'll be a great villain," Sterling says, almost salivating.

"She is fun," Dad says, wiping his cheeks. "Too much fun, sometimes. But not a villain. We won't be editing her that way."

Sterling starts, "Henry—"

"She's a friend. I'm not doing that to her. Unless she asks. She might like that. She's . . . mischievous like that. But, more importantly, she's ahead of us, so let's get in there and see what she means by 'put everything back exactly as I found it.'"

Dad and I pull open the doors to reveal the face of a startled nun.

"*Buon pomeriggio,*" she says, a little confused.

"Ciao," Dad says, then rattles off something in Italian. She shakes her head and points out the door, saying something, and Dad responds. They go back and forth before she turns around, leading us forward. We're in a tiny alcove, and she takes us into a tinier corridor. There are doors on either side, but she takes us to one at the hallway's end. Inside is a room too small for all of us. She nods us inside and then pushes her way back past us, going into one of the other little rooms.

"We won't all fit," Dad says. "Gabe, you film, and, Sterling, you go get some shots of outside."

"What did she say?" Sterling asks.

"That the lyre vanished centuries ago and was replaced with a box. She has it back here because Liat was looking at it. She thought we were with Liat."

"A box?" I ask, confused and sad. If the lyre was stolen, how can a box left in its place help us?

"She says it's been kept as a sort of artifact replacement. Nothing to do with music, but very ornate and beautiful. Let's look."

"I should go with you," Sterling says. "I have the camera."

"This room won't fit your camera," Dad says. "Here, you can go in and get a shot of the box, and then either you can take some exteriors or you can watch from the hall as we see if what Liat said about poison is real."

Sterling sighs. "Fine. Let me get some shots first."

She pushes past us into the room, and we hear a bang against the wall, then some twisting and a grunt. Sterling comes back out. "It's too small to even turn the camera around. I got a few shots, but . . ."

"We'll use the small cameras," Dad says. "That's why we have them."

Sterling frowns. "I'm starting to get that. I'll be outside I guess." She pushes past us again, leaving. The camera thuds against the wall as she turns to open the door leading outside.

Dad walks into the small room, where there's a simple wooden table against the wall and a bare bulb over it. On the table rests the box. Gabe and I crowd in around the other sides of the table, Gabe filming.

"Well, it's definitely old," I say, looking at the box. It's a large cube, maybe ten inches on each side. On top it's nearly blank; there are four small half spheres sticking out, and one slot, as though a final sphere is missing. Dad takes out a pair of gloves.

"Careful," I say. "Liat said there were poison needles."

Dad smirks. "She did. But that could have been a lie. For poison to last this long, it would have to be a very good mechanism, keeping the needle in a sealed solution—"

"Dad," I interrupt. "I know that. Still."

"I'll be careful," he says. He reaches for the box and lifts it. Nothing happens; no needles spring out to stab him. The sides of the box are much more detailed—full scenes in complicated three-dimensional overlays of metal, and a word is inscribed at the bottom of each. "Renaissance, I think." So it was stolen hundreds of years later.

"Is that French?" I ask.

"Yeah," Dad says, turning the box so we can look at each side. The one that was on top was the only blank one. The other five all have images.

Foi is written under an image of a young man in simple clothes who's holding a sling and facing a giant. Behind him, a king holds armor.

"That's David going to fight Goliath," I say.

"*Foi* is 'faith,'" Gabe says, proud to be helping.

"Gabe is in AP French," I tell Dad.

"Excellent. Looks like we might be going to France next." He turns the box.

Autorité is at the bottom of the next panel, which shows a young shepherd lifting his staff and sheep falling in line.

"'Authority,'" Gabe translates. "Like leadership. But you probably figured that one out." "David was a shepherd," I say.

Dad turns the box again. *Humilité*. A young man playing a lyre kneels before a king.

"David was King Saul's musician," I say.

"And humility is another, like . . . virtue?" Gabe asks. "Is that what we're seeing?"

"I think so," Dad says, turning the box again.

Virilité is on this side, which shows a man pulling a woman toward him. There are flowers behind them and, beyond that, a man walking away.

"This could be the story of Bathsheba," I say. "David saw her out a window and decided he must have her, so he sent her husband away to war, knowing he'd be killed. It caused a lot of problems. Not sure how that's virility, though."

"Aww, you translated it before me," Gabe says.

I grin. "Sorry, I didn't realize that was your thing. I promise you can do the last one."

"Virility could just mean spreading his progeny," Dad says.

"Maybe. But the first kid he had with Bathsheba died in childbirth," I say. "Supposedly as punishment for their adultery."

Dad shrugs. "He did have a lot of kids, though, right? So maybe this just depicts his . . . desire to propagate the species."

"His horniness?" Gabe asks.

"That doesn't always have to do with propagating the species," I say.

"Yes, sorry, turn of phrase. I'm trying not to get Sterling angry at us when she reviews this footage later."

I laugh. "Let's see the last panel."

Dad turns it again. *Fraternité*. The same man from the other panels, David, stands before another man, shaking his hand, their bodies close.

"'Brotherhood,'" Gabe announces.

"I don't know what scene this is," I say. "If this is some straight-washing version of him and Jonathan, then it should at least be accurate. Jonathan stripped to proclaim his friendship for David."

"My kind of friendship," Gabe says, elbowing me.

"Okay, so it's French, Renaissance," Dad says. "And I'm willing to bet from these . . . virtues on each panel that it's a secret order of some kind. Maybe chivalric."

"Chivalric?" Gabe asks. "Like knights?"

"Yeah," Dad says. "But also there were, like, secret, sort-of-occult orders that worshipped specific figures—in this case, David, obviously—and attributed certain religious, or pseudo-religious, virtues to them. The idea was to somehow embody these figures."

"Why?" Gabe asks.

"To gain power," Dad says. "Embody great men, become great men, but also have a secret society of powerful men to . . . I dunno, drink with. Start wars with."

"So pretty much like today," Gabe says. I laugh.

"Okay," I say. "So if each of these is a virtue, I sort of get it—his rejection of Saul's armor when he went to fight Goliath was faith in God to protect him, being a shepherd is leadership, humility is his performing for a king, him lusting after Bathsheba is—"

"Horniness," Gabe says.

"Yeah, that." I laugh. "And then brotherhood is him with Jonathan. Except . . ." I look at the final panel, then take out my own pair of gloves and put them on. I slowly reach forward, thinking of poison needles, and touch the surface of the box. Nothing happens. Each individual piece of the scene is its own panel, and they all seem to move on grooves or axes. Almost mechanical. I put my finger on Jonathan, and his clothing swings off, showing him naked underneath. Still no poison.

"How are they calling this 'brotherhood' and not just 'horniness' again?" Gabe asks.

"Stripping naked in front of someone was giving up your power to them," Dad says. "So symbolically, it's like two men pledging allegiance to each other."

"That's the straight version," I say.

"It's both gay and straight," Dad says. "Allegiance can mean a lot of things. It's context that matters, and you've proved the context to me. They were lovers."

I smile. "Thanks for the *foi*."

"Anytime," Dad says.

"So, Jonathan is naked now . . . the scene is right?" Gabe asks. "Should something happen?" He leans in with the camera.

I slowly pull the clothing off Jonathan as far as it will go, and suddenly there's a click as a small orb rolls out from under where his clothes are now.

"You think no one figured this out for all these years because the nun didn't want to take his clothes off?" Gabe asks.

I laugh. "No idea," I say, taking the small orb off the surface of the box. Dad turns the box back to the plain side that had been on top with the one empty groove. I put the orb in the groove, and there's immediately another click. I pull my hand back fast. The box vibrates slightly as the side with the half spheres pops up. Dad puts the box back down and lifts off the now-open top. Inside . . . is a letter.

"Okay . . . ," I say, reaching out and carefully looking at it. It's written in French, and there's a red wax seal at the bottom as a signature. The seal shows the same five half spheres like the box, but in the center of them is a lyre and a crown. "A secret society devoted to David, just like we guessed." I hold it up for Gabe to film so we can look at it later if needed. "Can you read it?"

"Kind of," Gabe says. "It's not modern French at all, but it's similar enough . . . It says, 'Sorry we took your lyre, we're leaving you this puzzle box, which is worth more and can help you understand . . .' like . . . 'truths,' I guess? And they say it's their job to protect David's legacy. And it's signed . . . 'the Order of King David.'"

"Well," Dad says, scratching his head. "This has gotten even more complicated."

"Yeah," I say.

"We should go back to the hotel. It's late. We can wash up, maybe eat, and then . . . figure out where this order was located."

"How?" I ask.

"Maybe the seal," Dad says. "Get a good photo of it. These kinds of symbols have been found, sometimes hidden, in all kinds of old documents, and we know it's French, so we can go from there."

"Should we close the box back up?" Gabe asks. "That's what Liat did, right?"

I think of Father Eriksen. Liat may have a lead on us, but I don't think the Vatican does.

"Let's close it all the way," I say, taking all five of the little spheres out of the top of the box. "There must be a place for each of them."

It takes a while, but we manage to completely lock it—each sphere was attached to something that, when pushed back into place, was wrong somehow. David is wearing the armor instead of King Saul holding it, the sheep are wandering and disorganized, David is standing as he plays for Saul, and Bathsheba's husband is positioned between her and David. I don't know how long it'll stall anyone who knows the stories, but I'm hoping maybe a little.

When we leave, Sterling is outside, talking in stilted Italian to the nun.

"*Grazi*," Dad says to the nun, walking away. Sterling quickly nods and follows.

"I was trying to ask her how she feels about your theory," Sterling says, quickly following.

"Who cares?" I ask.

"What did you find?" Sterling says instead of answering.

"A secret society devoted to King David stole the lyre, and now we have to go to France, but we don't know where in France yet!" Gabe says, it all bursting out of him. "I got great footage. There was a puzzle box, and it had all these panels. It was so cool."

"Wow," Sterling says, almost not believing it. "So . . . France next?"

"The hotel next," Dad says. "It's late, I haven't showered in two days, and I would like to have a nice dinner."

"Same," I say.

The hotel, once we're actually inside it, is gorgeous. Old stone walls painted with historical scenes, cracked but more beautiful because of it. Dad makes sure we have dinner reservations at the hotel restaurant for seven, and we head up to our rooms. In Gabe's and mine, which has a dark red carpet and blue walls, I immediately strip and hop in the shower. The stall is big enough that Gabe quickly joins me. He kisses me firmly, his tongue sliding into my mouth as he pushes me gently against the wall.

"Thank you," he says.

"For what?" I ask.

"Bringing me along. Letting me help with that box."

"You don't need to thank me. I like having you here," I say, wrapping my arms around him as the water pours down on us. "And not just for this naked part."

He grins. "But you do like the naked part, right?"

"I dunno," I say. "Just started. Let's see where it goes."

After we're out of the shower and lying in bed, wearing our hotel robes, I take out my laptop and start searching for the Order of David. The symbol comes up on a bunch of stuff, mostly in France.

"So, I have a question," Gabe says, making me look up.

"Yeah?"

"What are you going to do with the lyre if you find it?"

"Yeah." I sigh. I've been wondering about that a little myself. "Everyone will want it, I think. There'll be no shortage of options. But it's about who it belongs to and who's not going to straightwash it."

"Who does it belong to?"

"I mean, David and Jonathan were Jews who lived in Jerusalem, which is why the lyre was there, but by the time it was stolen, Jerusalem had already been under the rule of Greeks, Romans, Christians, Muslims, and was being invaded by Christians again. Most of the Western world would lay claim to a treasure of the Old Testament. So I feel like, heritage-wise, almost anyone can claim it, but since David and Jonathan were Jewish, and . . . let's be honest, so am I, I'd want Jews to have it. But more than that, I'd want queer people to have it."

"Is there a queer Jewish museum somewhere?" he asks, grabbing his phone and looking it up. "No," he says after a moment. "Lots of Jewish museums are doing exhibits on gay Jews, though—and that museum in Berlin—"

"Schwules?"

"Yeah. It's done exhibits on Jewish stuff before."

"Okay," I nod. "Maybe Schwules, then. There's a strong Jewish community in Berlin, too. Plus I know a curator there." I smile, thinking about Anika, my old boss at the museum back home. She was a visiting curator from Berlin who's back at Schwules now. I should email her.

"See?" Gabe says, putting his phone down. "Easy."

"I guess so." I feel a slight shiver from it, like I'm nervous.

"What?"

"It's . . . this will sound wild, but I'm trying to remember what our contract says about where the artifacts go. I'm pretty sure it says we get to decide, but the network gets access to filming, like, launch events, but now I'm worried I might have missed a clause where it says the network has approval or something." I try to remember going over it with Mom, every detail, but it was a long contract. Some of it is foggy.

"I don't think your dad would ever allow that."

"Yeah." That's true. And Mom would have seen it, too. It's fine. "Wow, all this is just getting in my head so much. It's like I can't focus."

"I think you need to remember what you love again," he says, taking my phone and opening up TikTok. "Time for a video."

"I'm in a bathrobe."

"So from the neck up. Talk about what we're doing, what you love."

I take the phone, smiling. I mean, what I love is finding the history, sharing the history. And we're doing that, or we will be. I know we're going to hunt down the lyre; I can feel it calling to me, my whole body pulled to it like a magnet. It was like this with the rings, too. But Sterling keeps making me forget that. I keep worrying. Gabe is right. I open up TikTok and look at the comments, trying to find a question to answer.

Except the first comment I see is *"Dude, why are you even doing this? No one cares about homo history."*

I frown. Rage suddenly slams through me like a stone slab, hitting me full in the chest. No one cares?

I start up a video, making sure I'm decent in the camera's viewfinder, and Gabe scoots to the side, out of view.

"So, I try not to read too many comments," I say to the camera, "but I just opened up TikTok and saw this one." I'll put in a shot of the comment after, but for now I point at the air. "So . . . why do I bother? Honestly, that's something I sometimes need to remind myself of. And it's not just that history is important or that our history is often overlooked. Especially now, as teaching gay history is actually being forbidden in schools. Because to me, that's like trying to make queer people feel alone. Like, I love both my parents; they're great. But they're straight. And so I can hear about the Jewish diaspora and my history with that from my mom. Or on my dad's side, I hear all these stories about my ancestor who was one of the first Americans to go west, searching for gold, so I have that connection, too. But neither of them can tell me stories of my queer ancestors—how I fit into that. So in my queerness, I sort of felt like I didn't really belong with my family. Even though my parents were both great when I came out, I felt alone." I shrug, then look away for a moment, feeling bad saying that, like it's somehow my parents' fault, but it isn't. Society is built to help people raise straight kids, not gay ones.

"I felt like I was the first queer person ever, because I had no history. And that's what I don't want people to feel. There's power in having a past, and it's a power a lot of people take for granted. Here's my family. Here's what we did. Here's the family tree I made in kindergarten to get a sense of who I am and where I come from. But queer history—where do we put that on our tree? By finding my queer ancestors, by seeing that I am nowhere near the first queer person and definitely not the last, I can see that part of my past. I can see that anything I've had to do, another queer person has had to do something similar, and they survived. And that's huge." I spread my arms wide. "That gives me a whole army at my back. So I'm not alone anymore. And if you're straight, then you seeing my history means you can show your kid queer history if they're queer, too, like my dad did with me." I nod and involuntarily smile, thinking of my dad. He's not perfect, but he handled my coming-out perfectly. "Yeah, I think that's actually a huge part of it, what my dad did. I want everyone to have their history, to know the past has their back, the way Dad did with me. So that's why I do it. And if you think that's not important, or that no one cares, you can just crawl right back under whatever rock you came out from, because I'll tell you what no one cares about: your opinion."

I stop filming and let a wave of happiness course through me like a sugar high from eating a whole pack of Twizzlers too fast. That felt good. Like I was in control of my own story again instead of Sterling and her branding and audience concerns. I shake my head. I don't do this for her. I don't do it for the network or Thrill or whatever made-up audience she thinks I can capture. I do it for myself, and for the other kids like me, who want to feel their history supporting them.

"Thanks," I say to Gabe. "I feel a lot better."

"I can tell," he says, smiling. He's been looking at his tablet while I record, his earbuds in. I finish the video and upload it, and he takes out his earbuds and looks at me.

"Wanna see what I've been working on while you research?" he asks, holding up the tablet.

"Yes."

He shows me a video. It's a man playing a lyre. "I'm teaching myself how to do it.

There's an app, too, a sort of fake one you can play on your phone."

"That's really cool," I say, feeling slightly worried. "But you know when we find it, you can't—"

He kisses me on the cheek mid-sentence. "I know. I'm not going to try to play an ancient artifact or anything. I doubt the strings will even still be on it, unless they're, like . . . replaced. They would have decayed ages ago. So no playing the priceless historical relic. No need to tell me."

"I mean . . . maybe with gloves. Curators do play historical instruments sometimes, you just have to handle it right."

"Oh?" He rolls over suddenly, on his hands and knees over me, his robe falling open in the process. He's not wearing anything underneath, and I smile. "How would you say my handling skills are?"

"Very good, in my experience, but it's always smart to practice more."

"Well, I think we have a little more time before we have to get down to dinner, right?"

"Absolutely," I say, reaching up and pulling him down into a kiss.

❧ SIX ❧

The hotel restaurant is small, with a bar on one side and only a few tables.

"We have a reservation for three," Dad says to the maître d', then he turns to me.

"Sterling said she had to eat in her room so she could talk to her boss and upload the dailies."

"The lady changed it back to four," the maître d' says, making me frown. I had a brief moment of joy knowing we'd be free from Sterling.

"She did?" Dad asks.

"I did," says a voice from behind us. I turn. Liat. Not in her sensible hiking boots anymore, she's now in a sleek red jumpsuit with a plunging neckline. Earrings dangle down either side of her long neck. "Hope you don't mind. I hate eating alone."

"You going to steal my wallet again?" Dad asks.

"What for? Your fancy network covers dinner, right? I just won't insist on splitting the check." She grins, and I can't help it—I grin back. Then I see Dad smiling, too, in a way that is very different from me, and I stop. I don't mind if Dad wants to sleep with her—I assume he's done it before. He has a lot of lady friends who seem to like his terrible flirting. But she's our competition. I worry about what he might let slip if she asks him while naked.

The maître d' shows us to a table in the corner, one flanked by faded murals of a lion and a deer staring each other down. Liat takes a seat next to Dad, then motions for me to sit on the other side.

"I want to know everything about you," she says. "That your dad hasn't told me already, I mean. He used to brag about you when you were little."

"He was barely around when I was little," I say, and Dad flinches. "It's okay," I say quickly. "You were having adventures."

"Well, your mom used to send him updates and photos," Liat says. "And he'd show them to me. There was one night, we were—where was it? Mount Ararat? We were camping out, but he'd downloaded all these photos before we left, and he just flipped through them on his phone, showing them off, saying stuff like, 'He's got trowel technique down and he's only three' about a photo of you in the sandbox." She laughs. "It's really nice to finally meet you."

"You too," I say, tilting my head. She seems sincere for once. "Though I'm sorry we have to find the lyre before you do."

She laughs. "Yep, definitely Henry's son."

We look at the menus and order when the waiter comes over. He brings a bottle of wine, and sodas for Gabe and me. I look at the bottle and wonder if it's too big for just two people, but Liat downs half her glass before the waiter is done pouring Dad's, so . . . maybe not.

"Oh, I needed that. I love this job, don't get me wrong, but I hate the parts when we get crammed on planes or in cars and just . . . travel. I want to be out there hiking it all."

"You should," Dad says. "You should hike to the next destination."

"France?" she says, raising an eyebrow. "If that was a test, it was a bad one, Henry. You can just ask me what I know if you want. I'm glad to exchange information."

"I'm not sure we can trust you," Dad says.

"She did just give us France," Gabe says. "She doesn't know we cracked the cube."

"She could have assumed," I say.

"I did assume," Liat says. "That's why I said it. I knew I wasn't giving anything away. Really, there's no need to be so suspicious. I won't lie about anything, I promise. I was a rabbi, you know."

"Dad said." I nod. "But you were bored, so you came to him to learn to be an archaeologist."

She smirks and looks at Dad. "Is that what I did?" She sips her wine.

"That's how I remember it."

"I was a resource at first," she says, turning to me. "One of these pretty researchers your dad knows so many of. I was a rabbi, yes, but I didn't actually oversee a congregation. I don't like talking in front of people or giving them advice on what to do with their lives. What I like is the history, and in Judaism, our history is all about discussion. We interpret and reinterpret and tell stories over and over, but then argue over what they mean. We're a culture of debate. In the Talmud, God even loses a debate and says his children have triumphed over him. Though

I guess 'loses' isn't entirely accurate . . . It's really more—" She pauses and smiles, raising her glass of wine and swirling it. "Well, as you can see, that's what I loved. So getting up in front of an ark and talking about the meaning of something . . . I could talk about what other, older rabbis have said about the history, but when it came to my own opinions, or what I thought the correct opinions were . . . I realized they were sort of empty. I loved absorbing, and learning, even arguing. I didn't love lecturing. So I stopped that part and became a researcher at a Jewish museum on the Lower East Side in New York. I studied turn-of-the-century Jewish immigration to the US, the late 1800s and early 1900s. Which is why your dad came to me when he was looking for a particular shofar that supposedly came through the city."

"The Sarug Shofar," Dad says, his eyes far away for a moment. "Originally made by a sixteenth-century Kabbalist. Supposedly anyone who heard it would see angels. The thought was that Sarug's descendants had kept it for centuries while traveling from Italy to Germany and then the United States."

"I helped Henry track those relatives and specifically look for notice of the shofar, but . . . I couldn't just give him the information and let him go. For one, this goy searching for a Jewish relic felt off, but also . . . I had to see how it would turn out. So I asked to go along."

"Begged."

"Asked very convincingly," Liat says, raising an eyebrow. "We never found it. The relatives moved from New York out west, to Chicago, but the records there were lost in a fire. We have no idea what happened to it. It could have burned, too."

"But by then she had the bug," Dad says proudly. "She wanted to find something."

"I did. It was only fair. So he took me on the next adventure, and the next, until we actually found something—the Champlain Compass—in a strange mountain stronghold on Mount Logan."

"I don't know that artifact," I say, looking at Dad. "Was it . . . ?"

He shakes his head. "Not like that."

"Nothing magic, you mean?" Liat asks.

I look at Dad, surprised. We edit that stuff out. Most people who know about it try to keep it secret.

"I've been around," Liat says, seeing my expression. "I know some objects do things they shouldn't. Like I'm guessing those rings of yours did."

"Yeah," I say.

"I know your dad is coy about it on the show. You think the lyre does anything?" She raises her glass to her lips, her eyes dancing between me and Dad.

"I haven't read anything to imply it was magic," I say. "Just special. A lover's gift."

She nods. "We agree on that."

"I'm glad. Mariana did not."

"Oh, Mariana's a pill," Liat says. "Ignore her. Ancient Judaism was well aware of homosexuality. Jews didn't love it, but Judaism didn't condemn it. Jews were supposed to have kids—so as long as they did that, the rest of it . . . varied from family to family. David and Jonathan both had kids. And they both loved each other, too. I think that's obvious from even the most basic reading of any of the texts. Stripping naked may be about prostration and allegiance, but not in the way it's described there. Not with the words they used, like love."

"Exactly," I say, smiling.

The waiter brings over our food, and we start eating.

"So where in France are you headed?" Liat asks, staring at Gabe, who frantically looks at me.

"Liat," Dad says, his voice a warning. "Be good."

"I'm just here for the ride," Gabe says. "I wanted an adventure—like you did."

Liat grins. "Well, I'm glad you're getting one. And you can't blame a girl for trying, right? You do a reverse image search for the seal yet? The results are pretty wild . . ." She takes another bite of her food.

"We got back and showered," I say. "I was going to do that after dinner."

"You want to know what I found?" she asks, leaning toward me. "Don't worry; no tricks. I know you can confirm everything I say, anyway."

"Sure," I say.

"Good, 'cause I love this part. Honestly, the worst thing about doing this now is doing it alone. I miss being able to talk over theories, figure stuff out together with your dad."

"You do?" Dad asks.

She ignores him, still talking to me. "So what I found is that the symbol was literally all over France for, like, twenty years—from 1750 to 1770. It was on orders from fancy courtiers, artists, priests. And then it narrows down fast, practically vanishes."

"Practically?" I ask.

She wiggles her eyebrows and takes a bite of her food. She's not giving me more than that.

"Wait," I say. "If this was your favorite part, the talking it over, the teamwork, then why'd you stop working together?"

Dad leans in, curious, too.

"The show," she says. "I don't want . . . When you're on TV, when people are looking at you—it's like being up in front of the ark again. I like the research, the adventure, not the explaining why something is important. It's history! It's important. I shouldn't need to explain beyond that. And then there was the whole advertising thing. That terrible trail mix your dad had to do those hokey turn-to-the-camera bits for."

"Yeah," I say.

"Just made my skin itch, the idea of being filmed, turned into this symbol, as opposed to a person."

"I get that," I say, thinking of Gabe and me juggling sunscreen. We were having fun in that moment, but to Sterling and Thrill and everyone else watching, we weren't two friends anymore. We were a symbol: the cute gay couple using Thrill sunscreen.

"When you're you, and you're with friends, you get to be complicated. On TV, you get turned flat, edited into something for viewers. They're never going to know you." She points at me with her fork. "They're only going to see you this one way. I hated that. It's a trap. Like, the first time someone came to me after services and asked for advice, called me 'Rabbi,' looked at me with those eyes that saw me as . . . something more, and less, than what I was . . . I knew I hated it. So I couldn't do the show. Same thing."

"You said you'd give Sterling a waiver to be on this season," Dad points out. "You didn't mind that."

"A cameo where I get to be fun and flirty and then gone? That's barely anything, and it's small enough that I can control it."

"You saying you're not fun and flirty?" Dad asks, a smile on his face that makes me roll my eyes.

"I'm not *just* fun and flirty," she says, leaning toward him. "I'm a lot more."

"I know," Dad says.

I clear my throat, and they glance up, Dad looking mildly embarrassed.

"Should we get dessert?" Gabe asks.

"Oh, yes," Liat says, leaning back from Dad but still smiling at him. "I love a sweet ending."

"Sterling wants to turn you into the villain," I say, wondering if she'll still feel like she can control how she appears on the show.

She smirks. "She can try if she wants."

"I told her no," Dad says. "Or at least not without your permission."

Liat tilts her head back and forth. "I think no. That's . . . too much attention." She smiles in a new way, less like a performance. "Thanks, Henry." She puts her hand over his.

He puts his other hand over hers. "You know I'll look out for you."

They're quiet, admiring each other in a way that is somehow more horrific than when they were outwardly flirting.

"Waiter," I call out desperately.

We order, and they keep flirting over sweet, soft *crema fritta*, but thankfully, when we go back upstairs to our rooms, she goes into hers alone, saying she needs to be up early. Dad says we should do the same, and to try to get a little research done so we can figure out where to go next. I pull up my tablet, do a reverse image search, and find exactly what Liat said—the symbol was everywhere in France, and even in Italy and England, though not as much, from 1750 to 1770. Usually on notes left in similar boxes where other things related to King David were stolen, about a dozen objects in total. None were ever recovered, either, except a painting of David holding a sling, which reappeared in Paris in 1993. I feel like that's probably where we should start, but it's just a guess.

"This part is pretty boring," Gabe says, watching me on the tablet. "I'm glad I'm not filming it."

I laugh. "Yeah, let's just go to sleep. We can figure it out in the morning."

"Okay." He turns out the light and immediately takes his usual position, his head resting on my chest, my arm around his shoulder. Later he'll roll off me before my arm falls asleep, and I'll turn on my side, but I'll wake up with him behind me, his arm over my waist.

"I like her," I say in the dark. "I know she's the competition, but she's cool, right?"

"Oh for sure. She's very cool. That outfit alone, plus the lipstick that she must have put on just to leave on your dad's face? And she picked his pocket! So cool."

"She was right about the being-on-TV thing, the being a symbol, not being seen as a person."

Gabe readjusts, props his chin on my chest so he's looking at me, and I can see his eyes in the faint light from the cracks in the closed blinds. "Here's what I think: no one will ever really know anyone else. Like, you and me, we're best friends, we've had sex, we know each other pretty well. But I don't know what it's like to be you; you don't know what it's like to be me. We can guess, we can try to tell each other, but no one really knows. Even history, a lot of it is kind of . . . guessing."

"It's not guessing," I say quickly. "It's looking at the pieces, putting together the stories."

"Sure, but . . . you'll never know what it was like to be King David, right? Even if you could bring him back from the dead and have a conversation . . . he'd still be presenting part of himself, not all of himself. We never really know anyone else the way we can know ourselves—and no one else will know us the way we fully are."

"Okay . . . ," I say. He's not wrong. But I wouldn't call it "guessing," exactly.

"So everything is like that, right? Social media, TV . . . They're just . . . bad pieces of the puzzle. They create pictures where some pieces of you feel more important, or are fake, even. They're pieces with less information. Or wrong information. But you love what you do—you love telling queer people about their history. That is a real piece of you. You even manage to ignore the homophobia you get online just so you can keep doing that. So ignoring that people think we're just adorable? That they don't get our relationship, that they think we love a certain brand of lip balm? I don't get why that's harder than ignoring the homophobes."

"I don't know," I say. "It just feels . . . different."

"Is it worth it to be able to feel what you feel when someone learns something from you?"

I look into Gabe's eyes, and I think of all the people I met when I was a part of the rings exhibit. I couldn't tour with Dad for that—I had school—but in New York, I met so many people who'd seen the show and wanted to see the rings, and they were . . . touched. They felt like they weren't alone anymore. Even the Good Upstanding Queers (aside from my ex and his new boyfriend) told me how empowered they were by the show. Being queer, not knowing your history—you feel alone, like you're the first gay person to have your set of problems. But seeing all our history stretched out, how many of us there are, how we come in so many ways of being . . . That makes us feel like we're part of an army taking on the world. And if I can make more queer people feel that way . . .

"Yeah," I say. "It's worth it."

I can handle people thinking I'm someone I'm not as long as I can make them feel like they're not alone and help them realize how important queer history is.

"Then put on some lip balm and kiss me tomorrow," Gabe says. "That'll make Sterling's day."

"I can kiss you without the lip balm right now."

"You can, but it won't be the same."

"Yeah, but will it be worth it anyway?"

"It might."

The next morning, I'm just out of the shower when I get a text from my dad. I was letting Gabe sleep in, but he stares up at me as I read the text: *Come to my room ASAP. Alone.*

I frown. Alone?

"I gotta go see Dad," I tell Gabe, leaning down and kissing him on the forehead. "You should probably shower."

"Awww, I wanted to do that with you."

"I'm already showered," I say.

He shrugs. "So?"

He gets out of bed and walks to the bathroom, letting his briefs slide off as he does so. I watch, wishing I could stay, but head down the hall to Dad's room.

"Oh good, you're here," says Sterling as I enter. She's sitting in a velvet armchair that's more like a tube than a chair, and her arms are pushed tight against her body.

"Morning," Dad says. He's sitting on the bed, looking tired. I scan the room for any trace of Liat having visited, but I don't see anything.

"What are we meeting about?" I ask. "Why couldn't I bring Gabe?"

"Last night I talked to some executives at the network," Sterling says.

"Okay," I say, sitting down on the bed next to Dad.

"They watched the dailies—my footage from yesterday—and they have some concerns."

"Just your footage? We've all been filming. Gabe shot all the good footage with the box."

"Yes, but what I shoot is officially what they're paying for. If you choose to give us your stuff, that's wonderful, but I need to upload mine every night."

"Before we go over it?" I ask Dad. "We usually pick what people see—we edit it." I think of what Gabe said last night—we pick the pieces.

"This is not like when we were doing it ourselves," Dad says. "And I didn't think anything needed to be censored from yesterday. We still have approval of the final edit, so this is just raw footage to give them a sense of where it could go. They do get to weigh in, though."

"And they have," Sterling says. "As I suspected. They have algorithms and research about their audiences and your audiences and who they felt your audience was, and they're worried about the direction it's going. The network tries to appeal to a wide viewership, not just the more coastal types. The network higher-ups don't think of what you do as prestige television but rather fun, family-oriented, adventurous reality stuff with a queer twist. Think of that global racing show with the tasks and the puzzles—"

"That's not what we do," I interrupt.

"No one is saying it is," Sterling says. "Just that there's a lot of potential audience overlap we are hoping to capture. Middle America isn't homophobic the way it used to be! A gay teenager on TV with his straight Dad, doing masculine stuff without anything very sexy? That's great. That has wide appeal. But the biblical angle . . ."

"Still?" I ask.

"People like what they were raised to believe. Oscar Wilde is gay. The Bible is straight. And we don't measure success by how controversial a show is, or how historically important. We measure it by how many eyes we get watching."

"So you won't give us as much advertising, I get it," I say, glancing at Dad, who's frowning.

"You told us this already."

"I did," Sterling says. "But this is from the network. The higher-ups feel like they took a big chance on you, and that you're not really honoring that by . . . veering away from what they thought they bought. And they're not sure they see a place for this kind of . . . prestige historical television on the network."

"So they'll cancel us?" I ask.

"No," Sterling says, tilting her head. "Well . . . probably not. They already invested enough money for this first season, but if you're hoping to continue on with us after that . . ."

"So no season two," I say, glaring.

"Probably not," Sterling says. "And probably a lot less marketing and publicity. This is what I've been saying, Ten. This is why I've been worried. How many viewers we get matters. And the executives don't think people will watch you try to turn the Bible gay."

"I'm not turning the Bible gay," I say, standing up. "And people will watch! The same people who watched last season."

"Last season was you guys on some dinky cable network that runs documentaries about how aliens built the pyramids. We're a global streaming service with over two hundred million subscribers. The goal isn't to keep the same audience—it's to grow that audience." Sterling stares down at her hands. "Look, I'm just the messenger. We'll keep doing whatever you want—contractually, we have to. And we have the funding for this season, mostly. We'll have to do more Thrill advertising, I think, maybe something big for them, to make sure we get that bonus so we stay in the black, but the network won't be promoting the show like they would have before. There's no cover of *Out* if you want to keep going for the lyre."

I sigh and look over at Dad.

He shrugs, sad. "If they cancel us, it'll be hard—I don't know if the old producers will take us back. It depends on if the network wants to kill us or sell us off. If they want to kill us, then we'd have to start from scratch—new name for the show, maybe wait a year because of the noncompete clause?" He turns to Sterling.

"Longer. They can wait months to officially cancel you, and then you have a year after that."

Dad sighs. "But we can do it. We can take a year and use some savings to fund the next adventure, film it, not put it up for a while, and then maybe someone will want us. Or we can try to put it back up on the web ourselves, like when I started. It'll be rough, but it won't end us. So it's your call, Tenny. I promised you that, and I'm keeping my promise. I'm going to keep doing this, show or not—what's important to me is doing it with you."

I smile and hug him. He squeezes me tight enough I can tell he's worried.

So we have choices:

1. Do what the network wants and go to Wilde's tomb instead. Let someone else find the lyre—Liat, hopefully. Not the Vatican. Feel like I missed out forever, like I gave up on something.

2. Ignore the network, go for the lyre, maybe find it! Maybe lose the show in the process.

3. My brain strives for some third option, some secret twist to make out of this, but all I can think of is . . . ask Dad.

"What would you do, if you were me?" I say to him.

There's a long pause, and he turns to look out the window before turning back to me. I feel nervous somehow. Like my teeth are about to chatter.

"I'd keep going for the lyre," he says.

Sterling sighs and stands up, her face serious. "Okay. I thought you'd say that. But if that's what we're doing, you have to promise me two things."

"What?" I ask.

"Use the Thrill stuff. We need to earn that bonus so I can get you any marketing. I have some kits, bottles of everything. Just put them in your bag, use them as often as possible, okay?"

"Wait, does Thrill know about the lyre?"

She glances away for a moment. "Yes. They don't mind it."

"So they're okay with me . . . What did you call it? 'Turning the Bible gay'?"

"Tenny," Dad says.

"That's what she called it," I say. "And she said they'd have a problem with it. But I guess they don't?"

Her face is a little red now. "No, they don't. They love you, and they love that Gabe is here, and that's what they care about. That and using their products."

I smile. Maybe Thrill isn't so bad. "Fine, I'll use the Thrill products, but no more . . . telling me how to use it. Telling me how to act. It feels like you want me to be this image, this—"

"Brand?" she says.

"Yeah. I just want to be me."

"That's all I want, too, Ten. You being you, but using the stuff . . . Maybe I can get some more money out of them if we do a sponsored post on socials, too, some video or . . ." Her eyes drift off. "I'll talk to them." She stares at me again, suddenly, hard. "But no more pranks. That goes for Gabe, too. No eating the products."

"Okay," I say. "You said there were two things, though. What's the second thing?"

She sighs and gets a weird expression I haven't seen on her before. Worry, maybe, but not just worry over products. It makes me nervous.

"You have to find the lyre. If we do a whole season looking for this lyre and don't find it . . . honestly, the network might not even air the first season. The executives will put it off for a year, then say you didn't live up to your promise, and then cancel you without ever having shown anything."

"Wouldn't that lose the money?"

"It's better than embarrassment. Plus, if they cancel you without showing it, you become a tax write-off for the network."

I don't even know what to say to that. It's like a slap across the face.

"So we need to find it. Not Liat, not the Vatican, not anyone else. Us. If we do that, and if the season is exciting enough, then maybe, with the Thrill bonus and some sweet-talking on my part, I can get them to advertise it enough for people to know it exists. And if that happens, and it's a really good season . . ." She looks me in the eye. "I took this job because I loved every other season and I wanted to help you guys grow. I wanted more people to see you. I'm genuinely a fan. I know you don't believe it, but I am. So I think if new people watch, they'll be hooked. So maybe, if this season is as amazing as I think it can be, we can get a second season out of them. But it has to be a sleeper hit, a win in spite of them."

"Okay," I say with a smile. "I like that."

"So let's find the lyre," she says.

"I think I have a lead on that," Dad says.

"Paris?" I ask. "The painting that came back?"

Dad grins. "Exactly. We need to find out how that painting reappeared. Then we can find out where the society kept their stolen treasures."

"It was more than twenty years ago," I say. "You think we can solve a mysterious reappearance from that far back?"

"We can try," Dad says. "We just gotta go to Paris. Already got us tickets. Same plane as Liat so she doesn't beat us there."

"How do you know which plane she's on?" I ask.

Dad smirks. "I may have texted her after dinner, flirted a little, got some information."

"Did she get any out of you?"

"Trust me, Tenny," he says. I look him over. The lines below his eyes are deeper than I remember. He looks tired.

"Okay," Sterling says. "So, when's the flight?"

"We should leave in about ten minutes," Dad says. "Go pack."

Sterling frowns and rushes out of the room, me following her, hoping Gabe is out of the shower by now. Thankfully he is, and although he's lying naked on the bed, which makes me want to delay, I managed to tell him to pack 'cause we're leaving.

"Paris?" he asks, throwing on some pink briefs.

"Paris," I confirm. "You can tell your mom we ended up going there after all."

"Think we'll have time to stop by Wilde's tomb?" he asks. "Check it out?"

"Probably not," I say, packing up everything and slipping on my green jacket. "We gotta solve a decades-old art . . . un-theft."

"Un-theft?"

"I don't know what else to call it. But it's the next part of our hunt for the lyre."

❧ SEVEN ❧

At the airport, Sterling gives Gabe and me little Thrill sample bags: a few sticks of lip balm, sunscreen as a spray and a cream, moisturizer, hand cream, body lotion, and cologne. Each container is small enough to have made it through security.

Gabe spritzes the air as we wait in line to board the plane, then sniffs.

"Orange?" he guesses.

"The Thrill Men signature line uses orange peel, bergamot, and oak for a fresh and masculine scent," Sterling says from behind him.

"Sir, can you not spray anything in the airport?" says the guy who takes our ticket. He speaks in a heavy Italian accent. I guess he knew to use English because only Americans would be doing that.

"Sorry," Gabe says, putting the cologne back in the sample bag.

The man scans our tickets, and we walk onto the boarding bridge, where the line continues. Dad is in front of us, texting, a grin on his face.

"Liat?" I ask.

"She's in first class," Dad says. "She's making fun of me for flying economy."

"It's only two hours," I say.

"I think she just wanted to be sitting down so she can smirk at us as we walk past, maybe toast us with the free champagne," Dad says.

Gabe laughs. "Yeah, that'll be fun."

"Don't get too chummy," Dad says. "She's the competition, remember."

I hadn't told Gabe about everything Dad, Sterling, and I had talked about. I don't want him to worry too much—this isn't his show, his career. For Gabe, it's adventure, fun. I don't want him worrying about me the whole time. I know I should tell him, but . . . we just don't have time, really. I mean, sure, there was time in the cab to the airport, but I was filming an update on why we're going to Paris. I'll tell him later.

When we get onto the plane, as Dad predicted, Liat is in first class and toasts us with a glass of champagne as we walk by.

"See you on the ground," I say.

"No you won't," she replies. "First class gets off a lot faster."

I frown. She's right. And even that much of a head start can blossom into something bigger. I take a deep breath. We need to get the lyre or else we're done.

In our seats, Gabe and I sit next to each other with me in the aisle seat. Sterling and Dad are across from us. Dad takes out one of the smaller cameras and gives it to Sterling.

"Your checked bag is slowing us down."

She sighs. "I know, but—"

"I get that it's good for longer shots when we're on a train or a boat, to keep it steady," Dad interrupts. "But you need to be able to pull one of these out and get filming the moment something happens, okay?"

She takes the small camera and turns it around in her hands, nodding. Then she turns it on and points it at me.

"This is actually pretty nice," she says.

I smile, take out the Thrill lip balm, and put it on, waving at the camera. It doesn't taste great, and it's a little thick, like it doesn't quite work on my lips, but Sterling looks so happy filming it. Gabe, next to me, nudges me with his arm.

"Giving in?" he whispers.

"Everyone is going to see what they want to see anyway, right?" I say. "That's what you said. So . . . sure, why not try to get the bonus for marketing money?" I don't tell him that now we need it, or that this still doesn't feel great but that I'll do it so I can keep talking about queer history.

"You sure?" He narrows his eyes at me.

"No," I confess. "But I thought I'd try."

"No harm trying," he says, leaning on my shoulder. "What do you wanna do for the flight?"

"Research," I say, grabbing my tablet. "Wanna read with me?"

"Okay, but I get to pick the music," he says, pulling out his phone. He pops one earbud into each of our ears and turns on a playlist simply called "ABBA." I laugh. "It was useful last time, right?" It was. Leo and I used ABBA to time our movements across a floor of falling tiles.

"Gimme! Gimme! Gimme!" starts playing as we take off, and I go over the research again. The painting of David was done by a minor

French artist in 1615. It was commissioned by a wealthy textiles merchant for the chapel in his manor house outside Paris, and that's where it stayed until 1772, when the merchant's family went into the chapel one day and found it missing. More than two hundred years later, in 1998, it showed up in a crate on the doorstep of an apartment in Paris. Weirdly, the apartment belonged to Aaron Crémieux, a descendant of the original merchant who owned the painting. This means someone tracked the whole Crémieux family lineage in order to return the painting to its rightful owner. The returned painting came with a note apologizing for the theft centuries before, but none of the articles have a photo of the note, so I can't read it. That's what I want to do first, which is why we have to track down the descendant to whom it was returned: Aaron Crémieux. A little digging lets me know he still lives in Paris, in the same apartment that the painting was returned to.

He gave it to a museum, of course—the cost of insurance for a painting that old, even by a minor artist, would be huge. There are photos of it in every article, too. I pull up a high-res version so it takes up the whole tablet screen.

"That's pretty gay," Gabe says.

It is. David stands at the center of the painting, holding a sling and wearing only a thin piece of white fabric tucked around his waist like a towel. In front of him, kneeling and naked, is Jonathan, but David is lifting up Jonathan's face. They're looking each other in the eye, and there's faint light around both of them in an otherwise dark room. The floor is tiled, and David stands in the center of a pattern—five circles, just like the puzzle box.

I look at their faces. They're in profile, so it's hard to make out their exact expressions, but they really do look like they're in love. I know not everyone would see it that way, but it's hard for me to deny.

I hold up the image for Dad and Sterling, whose camera is up immediately, filming.

"I think the artist felt the same way about their relationship as I do," I say.

"Those expressions could just be about friendship or respect," Sterling says. "Why are you so sure it's romantic love?"

"Why are you so sure it's not?" I ask, maybe a little harder than I need to. She doesn't answer.

"History is written by the victors," Dad says, and Sterling turns to film him. "It's an old saying, but I don't know if everyone understands what it means. It's not just that the army who slaughters the other gets to tell the story, because stories live on all over the place in many ways. History is always there to find. But what the expression means is that the dominant authority, the people with the power, will deem one of those histories 'correct' and go about teaching it as history, as truth."

I smile at Dad. That's sort of word for word from an email I'd sent him when trying to explain more about why it's important to give relics back to their original cultures. He said he wanted to be better, and so I've been sort of helping him understand how to be better, and he's . . . taken to it really well. People might be flawed—Dad isn't perfect, and neither am I—but we can improve. You just have to want to, and he did, finally, after he got over his defensiveness. I'm really proud of him.

"Look at what's happening in public schools nowadays," he continues, now no longer quoting from the email. "People fighting over if we can teach about slavery, the Holocaust, gay liberation. That's insane. These things happened, but by not teaching them, we're making sure people forget, or disbelieve. Tenny taught me all this, and it took a little while for me to get it, but it makes sense. It's not about victors writing history; history is everywhere. It's about victors deeming one history to be the truth and ignoring everything else. History isn't one voice. It's a chorus. Like, the thing that I always wonder about is how we stopped teaching about the unionization movement. My dad was a big union man, a mason, and it was so important to us growing up, but kids today don't know much about it at all—that unionization is a major part of American history, that unions gave us the weekend and so many things we take for granted now. So I asked, 'Why do schools and politicians not want us to know all this? Why did we stop teaching the voices of unions?' And what I came up with is that knowledge gives us power. Same with Black folks, people of color, queer folks—it gives them power to know their history, and to know their battles, and how they've been fought before. History is power." He glances over at me and grins. "How'd I do, Tenny?"

"Great, Dad," I say, my eyes a little moist. "That was all correct, and great."

"I think we should do it all again in the hotel tonight, though," Sterling says, "with the good camera. Maybe we can give some lines to Tennessee?"

I laugh. "Sterling, it wasn't a script."

"I'm glad to say it all again on whatever camera you want," Dad says, smiling.

I lean back in my seat. I need more than ever to make sure we find the lyre now, because after that, I can't let the show be canceled. Dad's changing is so important. It'll show other people they can change, too.

"You okay?" Gabe asks as Sterling tries to convince Dad that I should have said part of his speech.

"Yeah . . ." I turn to him. Gabe should know the truth, too. "Look, I should have told you earlier, but . . . the network, Sterling's bosses, they don't want us going for the lyre. This could be our last season."

"What?" His face falls. "Because of—"

"Yeah. Audiences uncomfortable with queering the Bible. But Sterling thinks if we find the lyre and use a lot of Thrill stuff and just . . . make it a great season, then we still have a shot at being a hit despite them. And Dad, just now, what he said—I want people to see it. I don't want it to end."

"Then we'll find the lyre," Gabe says, taking my hand and weaving his fingers through mine.

"I just want you to have fun, though," I say. "Don't worry about this. It's not on you. But I thought you should know."

"I'm going to make it the best season ever, I promise. Also your hands are so soft," he says in a fake amazed voice. "Why, whatever hand cream do you use?"

I laugh, and my body relaxes a little. I look over, and Dad and Sterling are still arguing. I lay my head on Gabe's shoulder and close my eyes for what feels like a moment but must have been more, because when I open them, we're landing.

I grab my stuff quickly and tap my foot as we wait to disembark, thinking of Liat getting off quickly. But as we're heading out of the airport to grab a taxi, I'm pleased to see she's been held up—until I see who she's been held up by. Father Eriksen, his leather jacket over his priest's collar and his two goons lurking at a distance, has stopped Liat by the line for the taxis. He's talking to her about something. I almost want to find out what—nothing good, based on her facial expression—but we can't miss this opportunity to get ahead of her.

"Do you see?" Gabe asks.

"Yeah, but let's just keep moving. We can find out what that's about later."

"Think they're working together?"

Dad laughs. "No way. Trust me on that."

We wheel past them, Sterling's purple bags definitely catching at least Liat's eye as she quickly breaks off the conversation to charge after us. We end up just in front of her.

"We can share a taxi," she says. "We're all going to the museum the painting is in, right?"

Interesting. She's not going to the descendant to whom it was returned. Did I miss something?

"I think we're going to the hotel first," I lie. "Unwind a little, unpack."

She laughs. "Sure."

"The Vatican trying to buy you off, too?" Dad asks.

"Yeah. I told them I don't work that way. But they might try to go after USJHA—give them a donation to fire me." She crosses her arms. "I don't know if they'll take it."

Dad reaches out and squeezes her arm. "I'm sure they won't. The Vatican still has that menorah they won't give back, right? They don't want this put on display. Just remind them of that."

"I will," Liat says. "I'll call them from the taxi. Sure I can't ride with you?"

"No room," Dad says with a shrug and a fake apologetic look. We're next and pile into our cab, waving goodbye to Liat through the windows.

Rome was like a sunset, and Venice like an alley in the rain, but Paris is the most beautiful statue garden in the world. There are winding streets filled with motorcycles and traffic, and the Seine, calm and pristine, promenades through the city. Old buildings rise up like they've been laid out by a landscaper, every facade selected for its beauty, There are newer buildings, too, but those blend in like glass windows in a castle, old and new standing together to create the perfect picture. It smells like fresh bread and roses, and also like exhaust from the traffic around us.

"It's really pretty," Gabe says. Sterling has her camera out, filming everything we pass through the window on one side, but on the other, Gabe is looking out his window with wonder. "Look at all the artists." He points at people painting along the riverbank. "And there's the Eiffel Tower!" He points again, then turns and kisses me on the mouth. "Thanks for bringing me."

I wrap my arms around his shoulders and grin. "You're welcome."

The drive to Aaron Crémieux's apartment doesn't take long, but by the time we get there, I wonder if it's too late and if we may have missed him—he probably has a 9-to-5 out of the house, like most people, right? He lives in an old Parisian walk-up. The doors at street level are wide open, revealing a curved marble staircase. Inside, an old woman is sweeping the floor.

"Crémieux?" I ask her.

"*Trois*," she says, pointing up. She narrows her eyes at our bags but goes back to sweeping. We walk to the third floor and knock, hoping someone will answer. And thankfully someone does. He's confused and tightening his tie when he answers the door, but when he sees us, his eyes lingering on Sterling's purple bag, he's even more confused.

"Aaron Crémieux?" I ask, hoping I'm not bungling the pronunciation of his last name too badly.

"*Oui.*" He finishes putting on his tie. "*Qui êtes-vous? Que voulez-vous?*" He tilts his head, focusing on me. "*Vous me semblez familier.*" I look at Gabe, having not gotten any of that.

"He says you look familiar," Gabe says.

"American?" Aaron asks. "I speak a little English. What is this?"

"My name is Tennessee Russo," I say, "and this is my dad, Henry. We're archaeologists on the hunt for a lost lyre—"

"*Oui*, yes, Tennessee Russo. My son, he . . ." Aaron's hands flourish, and he says something quickly in French.

"His son's a fan," Gabe says with a smile. "He's queer, too, a teenager. They watched last season together."

I grin. It's always easier when everyone is Family. "I'm so glad," I say. "You want to be on this season? We think that the painting that was returned to you in 1998 is a clue to a relic we're looking for."

Aaron frowns and shakes his head, so Gabe translates.

"I'm sorry, the painting is in a museum now," he says, frowning.

"But there was a note with it," I say. "Can we see that?"

"Oh, yes, that I kept. It's a good story, I had it framed, come . . ." He motions us inside. The apartment is gorgeous, with crown molding and white curtains drifting in the breeze from a small balcony. "I need to call work and tell them I will be late. Please just be careful, and you must take a photo with me, for my son." He points at something on the wall, and I approach it. It's a handwritten note framed behind glass, and at the bottom of it is a seal just like the one on the letter from the puzzle box. It has a border, too, a thin black line that occasionally spikes at random places, like the person who drew it was flicking ink.

"Dad, look." I point and quickly get out my phone to snap a photo and then a small camera to film it.

"Definitely on the right track," Dad says.

"So this is the note left by the person who returned the painting," I explain as I film the note. "My French isn't great, though, so . . . Gabe?"

"Okay," Gabe says, stepping forward and reading aloud. "It says . . . 'We return this to you, with many apologies for the theft of this painting from your ancestors'—huh, there's a mistake, or maybe I don't know this word, the accent is in the wrong place, but I think it's meant to say 'mansion.' So '. . . theft of this painting from your ancestors' mansion many years ago. We thought we were keeping safe a piece of art that celebrated King'—well, it says *kings*, plural, which is weird, but—'King David.'"

"Maybe the person who wrote it wasn't a native French speaker?" I guess.

"Maybe." Gabe shrugs. "Anyway, '. . . safekeeping a piece of art that celebrated King David, but we realize now that it was not ours to take, and not a symbol of what we thought. It rested'—well, *rest*, weirdly. But— 'it rested peacefully in a great'—I think that's not right, either, but—'a great space which has eluded many a . . .' I don't know this one, wait . . . Oh, it's another wrong accent. 'Eluded many a hunter.' Weird."

"Very weird," I say.

"'We are so very sorry for the time away from you, we do not want it to stay unappreciated as if in a marsh . . .' There's another mistake there." Gabe shakes his head and continues. "'. . . Unappreciated as if in a marsh, and so we return it to you, to do as you see fit. We think it might be nice in a museum. We hope you enjoy it. Sorry.' And then it's just signed with the seal."

"Huh," Dad says. "So what does that mean?"

Sterling has her camera out and is filming the letter, too. "I think it sounds like they stole it by mistake, right?"

"Yeah," I say, "but then why keep it for two hundred years?"

"It's funny, no?" Aaron asks, coming back into the room. "The letter?"

"It's strange," I agree. "Thank you for letting us see it."

"You think it will help you find something else?"

"I hope so," I say, looking it over again and thinking of the last test the secret society of King David had set: the puzzle box. "Gabe, the accents and the mistakes—do they ever *not* make the same mistake? Like, a correct accent in a word once but incorrect somewhere else . . . ? I think I'm seeing that, but I'm not sure." I point.

"Yeah," Gabe says. "That's exactly what that is."

"You thinking it's not a mistake, Tenny?"

I nod. "A code, maybe. The puzzle box was all about moving things around that were out of place. These accent marks could be like that. Gabe, write down every word with an incorrect mark." Gabe nods and takes out his phone, typing into it.

"Exciting," Aaron says, watching us. "I am texting my son about it. Will you take a selfie with me? He will be very jealous he was at school."

"Sure." I grin and pose for the photo. "What's his name?"

"Hugo," Aaron says.

"Tell him I'm sorry I missed him."

"Okay, so here are the words with wrong accents," Gabe says, holding up his phone. "*Mansion, kings, rest, street, great, hunter, marsh.* Is it just me, or does that sound like an address?"

"An address?" I ask, not hearing any street numbers.

"Mansion of King's Rest, or Manoir du Repos du Roi, which could be, like, a building. Rue Grande Chasseur, which, if you add a *du*, becomes Street of the Great Hunter, or Great Hunter Street, and then Marsh, Marais, a neighborhood."

"That's amazing," I say, hugging him tightly. "You must be right."

"And they say AP French is useless in school."

"I found it," Dad says, holding up his phone. "King's Rest Manor. Says it's privately owned, dates from the 1800s."

"So . . . not the society?" I ask.

Dad shrugs.

"I guess we'd better go find out."

❧ EIGHT ❧

After thanking Aaron, we leave him texting his son and head for the Marais. The Marais is like a fairy tale, with cobblestone streets and ivy coating the walls of buildings. There are mansions with turrets, castles really, and smaller houses—still mansions, to my eye—with redbrick fronts and windows that reach three stories high. We pass a few parks with beautiful fountains twinkling in the sun, and it makes me want to dance in them. Dad buys us some pastries. Croissants, pains au chocolat, Paris-Brests—sugar in exquisite forms, because we haven't eaten in hours. I almost forget we're in a race; everything about being here makes me want to stroll.

King's Rest Manor isn't as big as some of the other houses we've passed. It's down a narrow alley—Great Hunter Street—and tucked back a little from the street, with a gate in front. It's three stories high, half-hidden behind trees, but it looks art nouveau, slightly asymmetrical, with one large window on the side, its frame sweeping into the door like a cloud. Sadly, a curtain is drawn, so we can't see inside. But it looks dark. I hope someone is home.

"Before we knock," Sterling says suddenly, "can I get some shots of you, Ten? Just with the house . . . maybe putting on lip balm?"

I sigh. "Now?"

"It'll take a minute," she says. "We need those ad dollars, right?"

"Sure," I say, and stand in front of the house, putting on lip balm for a minute as she films it and takes a photo.

"Remember, the vibe is young, cute, adventure," she says. "Try to smile more."

I smile with all my teeth until she stops taking photos.

"All right, thanks," Sterling says.

I turn back to the house, glad to be done with that. The gate is unlocked, so we go through, and the door has only one bell, which I ring. There's no answer.

"They could be at work, Tenny," Dad says.

"Maybe," I say. If we wait that long, Liat will catch up to us for sure. I try knocking, and the door creaks open. I stare at it, confused. "Did someone beat us here?"

"Liat?" Dad guesses. "Probably not."

"What about the Vatican?" Gabe asks. "Father Eriksen was talking to her, so they're here already."

"They didn't even find the puzzle box . . . ," I start to say, but I let it drift off. "That was held in a church for centuries. Damn." I push the door open. "Hello?" I call. There's no answer. There's some mail on the ground that's been pushed through the mail slot, but it's covered in dust. So is the floor—no footprints. No one has been here in a long time.

"It looks abandoned," Dad says. He turns to Sterling, who's film-ing everything. "Not sure about the legality of this . . . but . . . let's go inside."

I also don't know if it's legal, but if no one has lived here in ages, I don't think I'm hurting anyone to go inside, so I do. I try the light switch, but it doesn't work, so I take a flashlight out of my bag. It's a wooden foyer with a decaying red rug over the floor and a hallway leading to one door. It smells stale.

"Close the door behind you," Dad says in a low voice to Sterling, who's filming us. She does, and now we're in near-total darkness. The window we saw outside doesn't look in on this hallway. No window does. Only our flashlights and the light from Sterling's video camera cast beams through the darkness. Every footstep seems to make the whole house creak and dust fly up. It smells so old, so stale.

"This is creepy," Gabe says. "Why would the note direct us to a creepy house?"

"I don't know," I say. The hallway's walls are bare, except for the door at the end. It has a symbol on it—five small circles, like the puzzle box. "But I think we're in the right place." I shine my light on the sym-bol to make sure Sterling gets a shot of it.

"Ha!" calls a voice from behind us, and I jump, worried we're about to be arrested for trespassing or, worse, murdered by a crazed occu-pant. But it's just Liat, hands on her hips. "I knew I could catch up."

"How'd you manage that?" Dad asks as she strides toward us.

"You shouldn't have mentioned the address you were going to in front of Aaron. I told him I was trying to catch up with you."

"That's cheating," Gabe says.

"Not really," Liat says with a grin. "Maybe a little." She looks at the door. "Ah, David's Stones again."

"David's Stones?" I ask.

"I assume these circles are supposed to be the five smooth stones he brought to fight Goliath," she says. "First on the box, now here."

"That makes sense," I say, blocking the door.

"What?" She arches an eyebrow. "You're going to keep me out?"

I look at Dad, unsure what to do, but he just shrugs.

1. Stand at the door . . . until she leaves? It's not looking like she's going to do that. She'll try to slip by.

2. Fight her? There are more of us, but aside from that time I took on a private army while empowered by magic rings, I've never fought anyone. And Liat isn't a private army; she's just a rival relic hunter. And I like her, I think. I don't want to fight her, and even if we won, then what? Tie her up until we're leaving to make sure we still have a head start? I'm not leaving her anywhere.

3. I guess if we really want this to be about who can track the clues . . .

"Okay," I say. "You can come in with us."

"Really?" Dad asks.

"But," I say, "whoever figures out what the next clue is gets a head start. The other has to stay here or, like, go have a croissant for an hour. That's only fair."

She folds her arms. "What if the lyre is in there?"

"Just sitting in a house in Paris for hundreds of years?" Dad asks. "If it's in there, it's hidden, and whoever finds it keeps it."

Liat tilts her head.

"You did cheat by just asking Aaron for the address," I say. "We knew to go to him first."

She sighs. "Fine." She extends her hand, and I shake it.

"And I open the door," I say, nodding at Sterling. "For the cameras."

Liat snorts and takes a step back, her hands up. I turn back to the door. Who knows if we can really trust her, but this is the best option right now. The symbol glows under my flashlight, and I touch the five stones—they're actual stones, I realize, rocks embedded in the wood.

"Really milking it, huh?" Liat says. "Come on, those Vatican creeps are looking for this, too."

I nod and turn the handle. It clicks. Inside is a dark room, but a huge one, vast enough that it swallows my flashlight's beam. I walk in slowly, followed by the others, shining my light around with a gasp as I see what surrounds us.

The whole room is clockwork. Like the box but huge, it's a chamber of gears and engraved brass. A single orb hangs from the ceiling, bare except for five stone marks around it. Every other wall is covered in clockwork—gears and flat metal carved into murals. If this is the room the exterior window looks in on, it's blocked by mechanical pieces and metal scenes.

With a click, the door shuts behind us of its own will. The orb above us flashes on—it's a buzzing chandelier. The room glows larger than life, but I swallow.

"Try the door," I say. Gabe goes to it and pulls, but it's locked now.

"A trap?" Dad asks.

Liat goes over to the door and takes a few pins out of her satchel. She tries to pick the lock but gives up after a moment, pounding the door. "Barred from the outside somehow. I can't believe we fell for this."

"Why would it be a trap?" I ask. "A trap laid in 1998 that no one tripped for twenty-five years? Why?"

Dad frowns and locks eyes with Liat. "That's the year we went looking for the lyre the first time."

I stare at him. "So this is a trap for you?"

"We went into a tomb outside Jerusalem and came up empty-handed," Dad says.

"It was the first trip we took together after the trip we met on," Liat said. "We didn't really think we'd find the lyre. It was more . . . learning the ropes."

Dad grins, still looking at Liat. "We did have fun with those ropes."

She laughs.

"Ew," I say. "Well, if this is a trap, then whoever does have the lyre must have taken you seriously."

"It doesn't feel like a trap," Gabe says, looking around. "Like, if it were a trap, wouldn't they just throw us down a pit or release some poison gas now?"

"Maybe after twenty-five years, the gas dissipated," Sterling says, her voice flat. "I really wish we'd gone to Oscar Wilde's tomb."

I look over at her. Her face is terrified, and I feel a twinge of sympathy. She's the worst, but she also really didn't know what she was getting into.

"But look." Gabe points at one of the walls. It's like a giant version of one of the box's panels. There's a huge figure of Goliath, twice as tall as me and made of flat metal, almost like a shadow puppet. He's glaring, holding a sword, and staring down at a smaller figure of David. They're the frontmost pieces, but behind them are more layers of metal with holes and grooves, showing the landscape, armies watching them, the sun in the sky. "This isn't a trap," Gabe says. "Or maybe it is. But it's a trap we can get out of. It's a test." He turns to me, grinning, and I smile back. Even when I start to feel hopeless, Gabe can make me feel hopeful again. And he's right—we're not dead yet. Maybe it is a test.

"A test . . ." I stare at the metal figures, the clockwork gears behind them visible. "Well, it looks like they move. Do we have to make them move?"

"What do we get if we pass the test?" Liat asks. "A prize, or to live? Because if it's the latter, then I think we can probably just pry the gears apart, right? Get out that way. That huge exterior window must be around here somewhere."

"No, I think Gabe is right," I say. "And what's the harm in trying?"

"Well," Liat says, looking up, "maybe you haven't noticed, but the ceiling itself is connected to those gears. I suspect the harm in failing the test would be it coming down on us. *Kersplat.*"

I follow her eyes and see she's right—the ceiling is connected to the clockwork of the walls.

"So let's not fail," I say.

"How?" Liat asks. "We don't know anything about this secret society of David except that they really liked King David."

"We know when they were most active," Gabe says. "And where."

"Well, we can guess," Liat says. "But that's not proof. And even if it were, what would it mean?"

"Renaissance French secret society?" Dad asks. "C'mon, we can guess a lot. There were plenty of chivalric societies back then."

"And we know their symbol is the five stones," I say.

Liat nods. "All right, if we're playing along, then five stones mean five things, right? A secret society's main symbol isn't just going to be those five stones; they're going to say each of the stones means something, so—"

"The box!" Gabe says, surprising himself based on his expression. "The box had five sides, each with a virtue, remember? I mean, it had six sides, like a normal box, but only five had virtues."

"Yes," I say, kissing him on the cheek. "And each scene represented one of the virtues they associated with David. So . . . we have to use those virtues to get out of here somehow."

"Do we just have to move things into place again?" Liat asks. She stares at the Goliath wall. "I don't see anything wrong."

"Maybe it's already fixed?" I ask. "The box was." We look around at the other walls. They depict similar scenes from the box but not in the same way. On the box, the panels were like illustrations from the Bible. Little vignettes. Here they feel more like murals, filled with meaning. There's Goliath and David, and then there's one of David and—I assume—Jonathan embracing, though from the angle I can't tell if Jonathan is naked because he's blocked by David's robes. Another seems to show David leading an army. He stands on a hilltop, sword high, as armies charge toward each other below him. And finally, there's David alone, playing a lyre, surrounded by pillows, fruit, wine. He's relaxing.

"Faith, authority, humility, virility—maybe, or just, like, horniness—and brotherhood," Gabe says, checking his phone. "I took notes on the box."

"Good thinking," I say. "But there's only four walls."

"And the ceiling of doom," Sterling adds.

"And the floor," Dad says, looking down. There's no gears; the floor is made from wooden slats, but there's a border near the edge. Along the border, the same words Gabe just spoke but in French are painted in calligraphy over and over. "Five virtues again here. That just makes it more confusing."

"And all these images are right," Liat says. "Nothing here shows something wrong with the stories about David."

"Unless you count calling his relationship with Jonathan brotherhood," I say, staring up at the panel of them embracing. I move forward and try sliding David out of place, but the piece won't budge. It's on a gear—I can feel it—but the gear is locked.

"So it's a homophobic chivalric order," Liat says. "No surprise there."

"Can I ask you . . . ?" I start, turning to her.

She arches an eyebrow.

"If you believe that they were queer, then you know the lyre is important to queer history."

"Yeah." She nods.

"So why not make sure it's presented as queer history?"

She smiles. "I don't like the presenting. I mean, I get it—someone has to, and history can be interpreted a lot of ways, but I . . . want to read, debate, interpret, not lecture. Don't put me behind a podium again. I just want to tell everyone what I discover and let them interpret."

"But you're giving the lyre to this Jewish group. If you find it."

She nods. "It's part of Jewish history. A major find." She shrugs. "And they're funding me."

"So you don't care about how it's interpreted? How queer history could be erased?"

"Not erased. It'll still be there—you'll still be there. I just . . . I want people to see what they want to see." She looks away from me, at the wall, studying it.

"People see what you show them, or they don't. If the museums don't talk about the relationship being queer, then that omission will be accepted as fact."

She turns to the panel of Goliath again and reaches out to touch one of the gears. All this clockwork, all these gears and pieces constructed to move something forward, but they can only travel along the path that's been built. If we wanted, we could take them apart, create something new with them; the pieces all fit in different ways. Facts can be put together to tell different stories. If you keep labeling one gear "friendship" instead of "romance," then history's gears will move forward on that path and leave romance behind until no one believes it's there. Queer history is like that. It's one of the pieces people don't use, even though it's just as strong, just as valid. But the clockwork of history is constantly being laid out to tell the stories of straight people. Queer people are always just ground down by them.

"If you believe in showing all the facts and letting people interpret, you should show all the facts, right?" I ask.

"What do you want me to do?" she asks. "Call up the USJHA and ask them to make sure that the queer relationship between Jonathan and David is a key part of the exhibition?"

When she says it like that, it seems obvious. It's almost like she's hit me over the head with it. I'm surprised no one else seems to realize what she just said.

"Yes," I say. "Call them and tell them that Jonathan and David's love story and queerness has to be part of the exhibit—a major part. And you can tell them if they do that, the exhibit will come with a lot more publicity because of it being on TV and you partnering with some pretty well-known relic hunters."

She raises her eyebrows at that. Gabe laughs.

"Tenny," Dad asks, "are you sure?"

"Yeah," I say. "It's what Sterling's been saying this whole time, right? Publicity is what gets the history seen. Well, for a historian, I have a lot of publicity to give—maybe not as much as the network has been hoping"—I nod at Sterling—"and maybe not the right kind to get me on the cover of *Out* or something. We'll see. But what I do have is a lot more than most museums can achieve on their own."

"So we'd team up?" Liat asks. "Split the commission?"

"Yes."

She tilts her head. "Eighty-twenty."

"Oh no," Dad says, walking toward her. "Fifty-fifty."

Money is usually Dad's field, so I let him handle it.

"Seventy-five–twenty-five," Liat says, folding her arms and smiling at Dad. "Fair's fair. I brought in the client."

"We bring in TV," Dad says. "And we beat you here."

"Only 'cause that priest delayed me," she says. "Besides, you're famous; you don't need the money. I have a lifestyle I need to uphold."

"I've seen your lifestyle," Dad says. "It's not that fancy. We have Tenny's college tuition to think about."

"Like he won't get a scholarship anywhere he wants," Liat says. "He's a genius."

I blush.

"Fifty-fifty," Dad repeats. "Fair split down the middle."

"Sixty-forty," I say. They both stare at me, Dad surprised, Liat pleased. "It's what she was hoping for anyway, and it's fair, she did bring in the client."

"I suppose it's fair," Liat says, turning back to Dad and extending her hand. "C'mon, let's finish what we started decades ago."

"All right," Dad says, shaking her hand. "If Tenny can live with that, so can I."

"But only if the USJHA agrees to highlight the queerness in their exhibition," I say.

"Highlighting queer and Jewish history."

"I can talk them into it. There's only one Orthodox guy on the board, and he's modern Orthodox, pretty cool. The rest will go for it completely. Hell, when I mentioned I'd worked with Henry in the interview, one wanted to know if I could get your autograph."

"Mine?" Dad asks.

"Nope," Liat says with a grin. "His." She nods at me.

Dad rolls his eyes. "Come on, then. I'm glad we're working together, but we should probably try to figure this place out. Who knows how far ahead of us that priest is, if he's looking for it, too?"

"Yeah," I say turning back to the walls.

"So . . . I noticed something," Gabe says. "There's a switch."

"What?" I ask, looking at where he's pointing. It's in a corner of the room, where the Goliath panel meets the lyre panel. Just a small lever I hadn't noticed because I'd been staring at the images themselves. And below that, oddly, the seam where the two walls meet is rounded outward, like a tube. The tube is made from the same metal as the walls of the box, and it's only about a foot long, so it's easy to miss. The bottom of the tube is sealed, but the top looks like it might come open. I pry at it with my hands, but it won't give.

"Nice catch," Liat says, walking over to the lever. "Should we flip it?"

"What about the crushing ceiling?" Sterling asks.

Liat shrugs.

"Wait," I say, tapping on the tube. I examine it and the switch—they're connected. Flipping the switch will make the lid of the tube lift up, too. "This is the prize. There's something in here, I bet."

"So then we definitely flip it," Dad says, joining us around the switch.

"Okay . . . ," I say. "Me?"

"You're the boss," Dad says.

After I feel Sterling focus the camera on me, I pull the switch down with a click.

There's a sudden metallic clanking as the room begins to move. Every wall clatters to life, every gear spins noisily. And then, suddenly, a noise like knives being drawn comes from above us. I swallow and look up.

"I think I just peed," Sterling says, following my gaze. The ceiling has spikes now.

They've unfolded from the clockwork, their long points facing down at us.

"At least it's not moving down yet," Gabe says.

"Yet," Liat repeats. "We need to solve this fast. Did the tube open?"

I look at the tube. The top was flipped open by the switch, but under that lid is another piece of metal, not an opening.

"No," I said. "There's still something blocking it."

"So it's not the answer key," Liat says, her eyes fluttering to the ceiling again. Still not moving. "All right, let's look at how the walls are moving, then. Maybe that'll be a hint."

"And the floor," Gabe says. "Look. *Autorité.*"

He's right. In the border made up of the five virtues, the word for leadership has lit up everywhere. And also . . .

"Pegs," I say. Small pegs have popped out of the floor at random points. Flat and holding still, like soldiers, waiting.

"So . . . leadership," Dad says. "Leadership was David as a shepherd on the box."

"There's no shepherd scene here," I say.

Above us there's a metallic *thunk*, and we all look up. The spikes look back, hungry.

"I think it moved," Sterling says.

"Yep. Came down about an inch," Liat says.

I feel sweat starting to drip down the back of my neck.

"Ah, the old falling spike ceiling," Dad says, hands on his hips. He glances over at Liat. "My fifth. Yours?"

"Third," she says, somewhere between annoyed and amused.

"First!" Sterling shouts. "But it's not moving anymore, so can we make sure that, if it does, we're gone by then?"

We all stare at the ceiling a moment longer. It stays for now.

"Okay . . . ," Gabe breathes. He's scared.

I look back up at the walls.

"There's sheep on a gear wheel," I say, spotting one amid the metal puppetry of the Goliath scene. "It's not moving." It's just a gear carved with sheep around the center hole, but it's just staying flat against the wall as the other pieces move in front of it. It's not doing anything, just resting on a . . . "Peg."

"What'd you call me?" Gabe asks.

"The pegs. I bet that wheel with the sheep, we need to put it on the pegs on the floor, to make it . . . move?" I look at all the pegs, their layout—but I'm not sure of the pattern. There are only two pegs closest to the walls: One in another corner, by a rotating gear so low that it's grazing the floor. And one more right by our feet, under the tube.

"Here's another sheep wheel," Liat says, pointing at the harp scene. The background of that one is whirling in a hypnotic pattern as stars and clouds move behind David, his arms and fingers plucking at the harp. But there, sometimes hidden by a metal cloud, is another wheel.

"One here, too," Dad says pointing at the army scene.

"And I got one," Gabe says, looking up at David and Jonathan.

"Okay . . ." I nod. "I think I get it."

Suddenly there's another loud creak from above us, and we all look up, holding our breath. The ceiling has come down a few more inches.

"Then do something fast!" Sterling says.

"We need to take those sheep wheels off the walls and put them here on the floor," I say, pointing. It feels like my whole body is sweating now, every hair standing on end. "The pegs will hold them, starting over there, where the gear touches the floor, and bringing the gears over here . . ." I point at my feet, where there's a final peg under the tube. "I think if this turns, then everything stops."

"Then just use your hands," Liat says with a shrug.

I get down on my knees and try to twist the peg. It gives a little, but whatever it's attached to is too heavy for me to just twist. I shake my head.

"It needs mechanical power."

Liat sighs. "Okay." She looks up at her sheep wheel floating behind the clouds. She tilts her head back and forth, cracking her neck, her body starting to bob as she approaches the wall. She reaches out suddenly, her hand like a snake, grabbing the sheep wheel from its place on the wall. She pulls it back just as a cloud cranks by, narrowly missing her hand.

"Careful," she says, holding up her wheel. "Those pieces are sharp. Almost just lost a hand."

"Yeah," Dad says. "Everyone, be very careful. But we're each in front of a wall, so . . ."

I nod and turn back to my wall. Goliath. The sheep wheel is behind David's arm, which swings in circles as he sways back and forth. A few gears are behind him, making the scene move. The notches in them glint sharply. Suddenly, there's another creak from above. I look up. Another few inches gone.

"We probably don't have more than fifteen minutes," Dad says.

I swallow and look back at the wall, watching the pattern. The sheep wheel is most exposed when David is swaying backward and his sling is rotated down. I count. It's a moment of about one second. Plenty of time. I count how often it happens, figure out the timing to grab, then count myself in and dart out my hand.

The wheel lifts off easily, which is good. It's thicker than I thought, though, heavier.

"Got mine," I say.

"Me too," Dad says from his wall.

I look over at Gabe. "You want me to—?"

But before I can finish asking, his hand is out, around his wheel. He pulls it back. I watch the sharp blade of Jonathan's arm pass by at almost the same time.

"Ha!" Gabe says. "Got it."

"Be careful," I tell him. He nods.

"The floor's changed," Dad says.

He's right. *Virilité* is lit up now.

"So . . . what?" Dad asks. "We're looking for wheels with beautiful women on them? Bathsheba?"

"I guess," I say, scanning my wall again. "I see one with clothes; I bet that's *fraternité* . . . What do you think happens if we take them off in the wrong order?"

"I bet they're locked," Liat says. "Immovable."

I nod. That makes sense.

The ceiling creaks again. This time I don't look up.

"There's a wheel with a woman sleeping," Gabe says. "Could that be it?"

"Sleeping or sunbathing?" I go over to look. "Oh yeah, that's Bathsheba. Look carefully; she's only on, like, a quarter of the wheel."

"What about the ones we have?" Liat asks, shouting over the loud clattering of the gears.

"Should we be trying to put them on these pegs?"

"I think we should try to get them all first," I say. "Then we'll be able to see the whole picture, their sizes, how they fit."

"Yeah, okay," Liat says. She lays her wheel on the floor. We all do likewise.

"I see my pretty lady," Dad says.

Liat snorts a laugh.

"Don't be jealous. You're a pretty lady, too," Dad says.

"Don't be gross, Dad."

"I see mine," Liat says. "And don't you worry. I can handle your father. Besides, he's right—I am a pretty lady."

I look for mine and finally spot it hiding behind the crowds of people watching David and Goliath. Not too high up. I don't think.

"Got it," Dad says.

"Done," Liat says at almost the same time.

I study my prey, bouncing slightly on my toes. I can reach it if I extend my arm fully. But maybe jumping will help. I shake out my arms. The crowd moves up and down, and a gear to the left rotates with sharp teeth. I count again, bouncing. When I have it, I jump and grab, but my arm is higher than I thought it would be. I wrap my hands over the wheel and pull back, but the teeth of the rotating gear slice my thumb, and I cry out in pain as I fall.

"Tenny!" Dad is by my side before I even land, and Gabe is right behind him. My hand is ringing with pain. But I'm still clutching the wheel. I got it.

I look down at my thumb. Just a cut, not even very deep. It's like a papercut. I was lucky. It only stings. Dad is taking a bandage out of his backpack. In seconds I'm fine again.

Then the ceiling lowers with another sharp creak. Seconds are precious.

"*Humilité* is next," Liat says, pointing at the floor. "David's time as a court musician. Look for the lyre, maybe?"

"Yeah," I say, scanning the wall. I spot it quickly, behind Goliath. "The wheel has lyres patterned all around it. They're small, though."

"Humble," Dad says. "I see mine."

"Me too," Gabe says.

"Already have mine," Liat says, darting away from the wall.

Goliath moves slower, so this one is easier, and we all have our wheels in a matter of moments. Next is *foi*—wheels with unworn armor and a sling, for the faith David had that God would protect him. The ceiling lowers again, but we move quickly. Soon we all have our wheels again and are ready for the final round: *fraternité*.

"What would the picture be?" I ask. "Men kissing?"

"No, Tenny," Dad says. "I'm going to guess this secret society wasn't exactly gay friendly, based on the note from when they returned the painting. So while on the puzzle box, brotherhood was the moment where they stripped . . . I don't think that means here it's going to be men kissing, though I'd be very pleased and impressed if it were."

"I was kidding, Dad."

"Oh."

"Clothes," Liat says. "You said you saw a wheel with just a pile of clothes carved into it on your wall. There's one here, too."

"Right," I say. The noise and the falling spikes made me forget.

The ceiling lowers again, louder than before. I look up. If I reached out and jumped, I could probably touch the tip of one spike.

"Hurry," Dad says.

"Please!" Sterling adds. I glance over. She's been filming everything, walking around hunched over like the ceiling is already low, glancing up nervously all the time, but now she's by the door, trying the handle again.

Dad and Liat find and grab their wheels quickly.

"Start seeing if you can assemble something with them on the floor," I say, still scanning my wall for the gear. I finally spot it. It's practically on the floor, covered by other gears moving in front of it. Luckily, it's so low down that I can carefully pluck it without touching the other gears just by coming in from above.

Only one wheel left. I look over at Gabe, who's smiling, leaning back on one foot. He's about to jump. That's how I hurt myself.

"Wait," I say, but it's too late. He's in the air, his arm out. It's like slow motion, watching him grab the gear just as David's sharp hand comes down on him. He cries out. The gear drops to the floor.

So does he. I rush over. He's clutching his hand. "Dad, first aid kit!" I shout.

Dad is next to us in a second. Gabe's hand is bleeding. A lot. We wash the area with some water first, to find the wound. It's in the fleshy part under his thumb, and it's deep.

"I'm going to need to stitch it up once we're free," Dad says.

Gabe looks at me. His eyes are wide with fear and pain. I grab his other hand and squeeze.

"It's okay to scream," I say. "And it'll be a cool scar. Dad stitched up a cut I got from a trap in Morocco that one time, remember, Dad? You've seen it. The line on my thigh?"

"Yeah," Gabe says through clenched teeth. "That's a cool one."

"It should be fine. It doesn't look like it damaged any muscle or anything," Dad says. "We'll wrap it for now." He takes some gauze from the kit and wraps it tight around Gabe's hand.

"Thanks," Gabe says. "Sorry."

"Don't apologize. Drink water. Stay lying down. I'm going to try to put the wheels in the right places."

"No," Gabe says, standing. He wobbles, and I take him by the shoulders, but he gets himself up again. "I'm helping."

There's no time to argue. We hurry across the room to where Liat has gathered all the wheels and started assembling them. One wheel has been put on the peg closest to the wall, and it's locked with the moving gear there, so it's turning.

"I just don't see how these work," Liat says. "There are too many combinations."

The ceiling creaks overhead, and I don't look up. I can feel my heart racing, pushing so hard against my chest that I feel like it's trying to escape.

I look over the pegs and the wheels that are laid out, placing them each in my mind's eye.

"No, there's not." It's just like I was thinking about the clockwork. Gears could, in theory, be used to fit together in a hundred different ways, to power a hundred different things. Each piece of the story could be laid out to tell the truth from a different angle. But the folks who made this trap will see just one story, one angle—and the gears only line up one way. Their five virtues, the same images over and over—they've built a whole story for David that has no nuance, no room for argument—just the one story.

"Here," I say, kneeling and taking a gear. I put it on the next peg, connecting it so it interlocks with the last gear and starts turning. "It's just about the distance between each peg and the size of the gears."

"Right," Dad says.

The ceiling drops again with a clang, and Dad ducks.

"Felt that one," he says. I look up. The ceiling is low enough that if Dad stood upright, he'd get a haircut.

"Everyone stay low," Liat says. "We're in the danger zone now." She grins.

"Maybe we should . . ." I walk, hunched over, to where the final peg is. There's only one gear that's the right shape to fit on the peg here without also scraping the side of the wall. I go back and grab that one and put it down. "We can try working backward, too . . ."

"We'll work forward," Dad says. "You and Gabe work backward. It'll be faster."

"Okay," I say, getting to work. There's another screech of metal as the ceiling drops again. I gather wheels as quickly as I can, watching them shake in my hands, and try putting them on the pegs. It's easier backward, I think, because there are fewer wheels that fit if you're working that way. They laid this out to be difficult if you're starting from the beginning. But going backward, the sizes of the spaces for the wheels are a lot more obvious. They didn't expect anyone to even try looking at the story a different way.

When I meet up with Dad and Liat in the middle, the ceiling falls again. The chandelier hits the floor with a dull thunk, the shadows in the room stretching up from it dramatically. Now if I stand up, I'll get a spike through my head to the bottom of my chin. Dad puts the final wheel down, but it doesn't meet up with mine.

"Did we miss one?" Liat asks.

"Switch those two," Gabe says, pointing at the final two wheels each of us have just placed. We do, and then I see it and switch one more of Dad's with another. The ceiling falls again, and I swallow, going as quickly as I can. The ceiling drops *again*, the knives screeching closer. A few more switches and we're there. All the wheels on the floor are moving and . . .

"Now what?" Sterling asks.

There's a creaking noise, and all the walls stop moving.

"Okay," I say, taking a deep breath. My body is suddenly shaking. I'm drenched in sweat; my shirt is clinging to me and so wet that now I'm shivering. But we did it. We survived mortal peril. I hope.

There's a click from the door. Sterling crawls for it, unwilling to stand up and risk impaling herself, even though the spikes are still high enough that she'd probably be fine, being shorter than the rest of us. She pushes the door, and it swings open.

"Oh, thank god," she says. She might be crying. I feel bad for a moment. She literally signed up for this, but still, no one really signs up for being slowly impaled.

"Did the tube open?" Gabe asks. I go over to it, keeping my head low, and look at the tube. The second seal is gone. Inside is some rolled paper. I pull it out.

"Another letter?" Dad asks.

I unfurl it. "A map."

"To what?" Gabe asks.

"I guess we'd better find out, fast."

❦ NINE ❦

It's just a map of France. No markers, no clues that I can see. Nothing leading us to the lyre. I don't get it. All that for this?

"You're looking at it in a room where you have to crouch and the chandelier is on the floor," Liat says. "Let's take it outside."

I hold it up to the dim light of the chandelier to see if anything shines through, but there's nothing. I take a few photos of it, too, and film myself unrolling it on the floor for the show.

"All right, Tenny, my back is starting to ache," Dad says, heading for the door.

"And the ceiling seems to be holding . . . ," Gabe says, following, "but . . ."

Liat nods at the door, and we both go after them, coming back into the dark hallway. There, I throw open the door for light and air, and make Gabe sit on a dusty chair, telling Dad to get the first aid kit out again.

Dad takes out the needle and thread. First he dabs alcohol on the wound, and Gabe shrieks. Then the sewing starts. Gabe groans more than screams through that. I clutch Gabe's free hand in mine, letting him squeeze it, holding the map in my other hand. When the stitching is done, Dad puts some pain cream over the wound and wraps it up in gauze.

"Cool scar, right?" Gabe asks, his voice weak, face slick with sweat.

I give him some water. "Cool scar," I promise. I hope this map was worth it. It curls in my hand, the paper soft and thick. It's old but has been well preserved in that tube. It's not crackling.

"So what is it?" Sterling asks, nodding at the map. She's got the camera up, and it's bright on my face.

"A map," I hold it up. Everyone else sees it for the first time.

"Well, it's France," Dad says.

"No markers, no route . . . ," Liat says, studying it.

"The border is sort of funny," Gabe says, pointing at the thin black line around the map. It's marked in a few seemingly random places with a small flourish, like the loops of fancy calligraphy.

"That could be something," I say.

"Let's get somewhere we can lay it out, compare it to another map," Dad says. "Research will help us figure it out."

"Yeah," I say. "And get something to eat. Almost being impaled makes me hungry."

Sterling laughs, too loud and long, at that. "Sorry," she says. "Trauma, I think." She lowers the camera as Dad pats her on the back.

"You get used to the thrills," he says.

"You learn to love it," Liat adds.

Outside there's a young guy, maybe my age, looking up at the building, confused. He's wearing a red leather moto jacket and has his hand on a motorcycle as he stares up at the house.

Another person after the lyre? But when his eyes fall down to me, he lights up and runs forward.

"Tennessee," he says in a French accent. "I did not believe it, but here you are." He reaches me and kisses me on both cheeks. He's pretty cute, with wispy blond hair to his jaw and bright green eyes, so I don't mind it. I catch Gabe grinning at me.

"Uh, hello," I say.

"Oh, apologies. I'm Hugo. My father is Aaron? You were at his house. He sent me a photo, and I did not believe it. I love your Instagram. Oh"—he spots Gabe—"and Gabriel!" He runs over and kisses Gabe on both cheeks, too. "Both of you. I did not believe it, but Papa said you were coming here, and I was done with classes, so I thought . . ."

"Oh," I say. "Aaron's son. Hi. It's great to meet you. You want a photo?"

It's a little weird that he stalked us here, but his dad gave us a hand, so I don't mind thanking him.

"Oh, yes, if you're willing. I thought maybe I could show you"—he glances between me and Gabe, then the adults—"all of you, that is, Paris. If you are not leaving so soon."

"We did just say we need to grab something to eat," Dad says, trying not to laugh at all this.

"Oh, yes, I know a wonderful café only a short distance. But first, can we . . ." He takes out his phone, and I nod, going to stand next to him. He motions to Gabe, who stands with us, and he takes several selfies with us on the sidewalk.

"So you watch the show?" Dad asks.

"Ah, well, yes, sometimes, but it's more his Instagram and TikTok that I follow. The little videos on queer history. They are so powerful."

"I don't even have a TikTok," Dad says, looking at Liat.

"Should I be surprised?" she asks.

An engine roars, and I glance at the corner, where a dark van has appeared and is barreling toward us. Drunk driver? I step back from the curb as it screeches to a halt in front of us.

The passenger door slams open, fast. A man in a ski mask grabs me around the waist.

"Tenny!" Dad shouts, running forward. Gabe swings at the man. The man dodges and pushes Gabe down. Gabe hits the pavement with a thud that makes me yell and thrash harder, loosening the man's grip.

Before I can get completely loose, though, he spins and slams me into the side of the van. I feel my head snap on the metal for a moment, my body tingling with the shock. The man looks at my hand, the map. Before I can react, he snatches it from me, my grip loose from the blow. Dad reaches him and grabs his shoulder, pulling him back. The man kicks Dad, who tumbles back onto the pavement. The man jumps back into the van. I stumble forward as he slams the door. It peels off in reverse, back to the main street it turned off.

"Are you all right?" Dad asks, rushing to me.

"He took the map," I say.

"Dammit," Liat says.

Sterling is just staring after the van, her camera stiff on her shoulder.

But Gabe is up and looking at Hugo. "Can I borrow your bike? I can drive it, I promise."

"Uh," Hugo says. He looks shocked. He glances at me. "You'll bring it back?"

"Absolutely," Gabe says, sitting astride the motorcycle. "Ten? There's room."

"You just got hit in the head!" Dad says.

"I'm fine," I say, nodding, and get on the bike behind Gabe. "You okay?" I glance at his bandaged hand.

"Fine," Gabe says.

"Tenny, no," Dad says.

Hugo hands Gabe the keys. "This is so exciting."

I wrap my hands around Gabe's waist, and before Dad can stop us, we shoot forward like a bullet, chasing the van.

I've never been on a motorcycle before. It's not like a bicycle. It hums between my legs like an animal. It feels like we're a blade cutting through traffic. We follow the van onto the main street, but it has a big lead already.

"I wish we had your helmet," I say. The wind drowns me out, so I repeat myself.

"I'll be careful," Gabe says. I don't say that I don't think that's possible given the circumstances.

The van hits traffic ahead, and I think that we might catch up. The wind at this speed is freezing and bites through my clothes. The cars we zoom between honk, the sound already fading behind us. I feel Gabe wince slightly under me and glance at his bandaged hand, which he stretches for a moment before tightening his grip on the handle. My heart is beating louder than the wind now. We just survived a death trap, but this is probably how we're going to die, I realize.

The traffic seems to clear, and the van turns and then seems to spot us, suddenly swerving around the cars in front of it and speeding up.

"Can you get the license plate?" Gabe asks.

I carefully take my phone out and hold it up, filming the van as we try to close the distance. We weave through cars and turn where it turns, our bodies leaning much closer to the pavement than I'd like. I almost drop my phone.

Gabe shoots forward even faster, but then we see the van turn again, into an alley. I realize I don't know what we'll do if we catch up. The man in the ski mask was big—big enough to push Gabe to the ground. And there must be someone else driving. Maybe we could take them on, but I don't know. My heart rises in my chest, and my throat feels squeezed tight. But I want to catch these guys, figure out who they are, and take back our map.

Gabe steers us down the alley where the car turned. It's narrow . . . and empty. He slows the bike down, cruising forward carefully.

"Where did they go?" I whisper.

Gabe shrugs, and I tighten my arms around him. I can smell his deodorant—orange, wood—mixed with the exhaust of the motorcycle. The alley reaches a dead end, so we turn back around. I spot another alleyway, smaller than this one. It looks too narrow for a van. I get off the motorcycle and go over to it. Black paint is scraped along the sides of the buildings. I run to the end of the smaller alley and look both ways, but there's nothing. We lost them.

"Damn," Gabe says as I walk back to him, shaking my head. He laughs. "Well, at least we tried. You get the license plate number?"

I look at the footage on my phone. I did, and also the clip is awesome and will look great on TV.

"Yeah." I show it to him. "But we're not police. We can't run a license plate."

My phone rings. Dad. I pick up.

"Tenny?" He sounds really worried. "You okay?"

"Yeah," I say, "but they got away."

"That's fine. You're safe, that's fine. Just tell us where you are, and we'll come meet you."

I drop a pin, and we lean against the walls and wait. I think about the man, the way he grabbed me so easily. He was huge, I think. Or was he? And who was he? Had they just been waiting for us? One of Father Eriksen's goons? Someone else after the lyre? Why did he know to grab the map?

"You okay?" Gabe asks. "I'm sorry. I should have driven faster."

"No, that's not it. I'm glad, honestly . . . What would we have done if we'd caught up to them?"

"Kicked that dude's ass," Gabe says. "Taken the map back."

I grin. "Think we could have?"

"Yeah." Gabe nods. "For sure." He thinks about it for a moment. "He was big, though."

I take his hand in mine and hold it tightly. "That was really brave, getting on the motorcycle."

"Yeah, but you're about to say it was really dangerous, too, right?"

"Well . . ."

"You do dangerous stuff all the time, though. We just almost got impaled by a spiked ceiling."

"Yeah," I say. He's right. "It's different. I don't know how to explain it. Just . . . I was kind of scared."

"That I'd crash?"

"No, *for* you. That we'd catch up to them and the guy would, like, shoot you or something. I was worried about you."

He smiles, small at first but growing. "That's how I feel watching you on the show, y'know. Watching you solve puzzles in that trap we just got out of. I worry, too."

"Well . . . you should tell me. I feel better now that I've said I was worried about you."

"I feel better, too, actually," he says, dropping my hand and putting his arms around my waist. He hugs me tightly. "We should always tell each other when we're worried, okay? Not to stop the other from doing something, but just to remind them that . . . if they die, someone else will be really sad."

"I wouldn't want you to be sad," I say.

"And I wouldn't want you to be sad." We keep hugging until a taxi turns into the alley.

It stops in front of us, and Dad, Sterling, Liat, and Hugo all get out before it pulls away.

"Oh, thank god," Dad says. "No helmet? I'm tempted to yell at you, Gabe. And I definitely want to yell at you, Tenny."

"I got on the bike," I say. "My choice. Don't yell at Gabe."

"That was way too dangerous," Dad says.

"We were all in a room of falling spikes together," I counter.

"That's different!"

"Chasing them on the motorcycle was very exciting, though," Hugo offers. Dad glares at him. "But illegal," Hugo adds quickly. "You must have a helmet. I should have given it to you."

"Thank you," I say, squeezing Hugo's arm. "We didn't catch them, though."

"We got a license plate number," Gabe says, handing Hugo his keys back and hugging him. Hugo is blushing bright red.

"At least we have a photo of the map," Dad says, scratching his head. "I just wish I knew how to read it."

"There could have been some chemical reaction we needed to do . . . ," Liat says. She looks down the alleyway, frowning. "But maybe we can figure something else out."

"Well, Dad always says that if you're at a dead end, go back to the last clue," I say.

"The room with the ceiling?" Sterling asks, nervous.

"Or the letter."

"Yes, the letter," Hugo says, excited. "Come back to our home; we can go over it again. Then we can all go out to dinner." He smiles at me.

I stare down the street. The sun is sort of low. I'm shaking—a spiked ceiling, sharp gears, a motorcycle chase . . . I'm drained. I need to eat.

"That's not a bad idea," Dad says. "If there was some sort of secret message in chemicals on the map, there could be something more in the letter."

"All right," I say. "Let's look at the letter again."

"We are right nearby now," Hugo says, getting on his motorcycle. "I will go slow. Just follow. Or you can . . . ride with me?"

"No," Dad says quickly. "No more motorcycles for you, Tenny."

I laugh. "All right. Lead the way, Hugo."

We follow Hugo as he drives ahead. He stops at every corner to make sure we're keeping up. We're walking slowly. Sterling has the camera to lug, but also . . . we're all tired. More than we'd like to admit, I think. No one says anything. Liat and Dad don't even tease each other.

When we get to a street I recognize, I feel a weird sort of relief, like maybe we can relax for real now.

Until I see the van. I stop moving and hold out my hands. When Hugo looks back at us, I wave him over. We duck behind the edge of a building as I take out my phone and check the license plate of the van we chased. Then I check the plate of the van now parked in front of Hugo and Aaron's apartment building. They're the same.

❧ TEN ❧

I show the video of the license plate to everyone and point out the van parked in front of Hugo and Aaron's apartment. Everyone's mood, which had finally started to relax, shifts again, turning jagged at the edges. This day has gone on too long. It's stretched out like old gum that you can see light through. I feel like that, too. Worn.

"What are they doing here?" Sterling asks in a harsh whisper.

"Maybe they had the same idea as us," Dad says.

"They're with my father, then?" Hugo asks. "We should call the police?"

"I don't think they'd hurt him . . . ," I say, but I'm not sure. I peek around the corner again, phone out. Two men come out of Hugo and Aaron's building. One's huge, like the man who grabbed me. No ski masks this time, but I don't recognize their faces. They're in their forties or fifties maybe, white, smug looking. I grab a few photos. One of them is holding something—paper. The letter? They get in the van and speed off.

"Should we chase them again?" Gabe asks.

I shake my head. "We need to check on Aaron. And we know what the letter looks like already."

Hugo hears that and dashes off, leaving his motorcycle behind, running to the building to check on his father. I chase after him, the others behind me. We run up the stairs. I said I didn't think they'd hurt Aaron, but what do I know, really?

The door to the apartment is open, and inside, Hugo is already hugging his father, who looks fine. They talk in French.

"Hugo is asking if he's okay," Gabe says to me in a low voice. "Aaron is saying he is. They just came in, demanded the letter, took it, and left."

I look over at the wall where the letter was hanging. The frame is on the floor, shattered glass around it like a constellation.

"I'm so sorry," I say. "I don't know why they wanted it, but it must have something to do with us."

"They attacked Tennessee and Gabriel, too, Papa," Hugo says.

"We are all fine," Aaron says. "There is nothing to be upset about. It was not valuable, just a silly little letter I thought was funny."

"But then why did they want it?" Liat asks. "They had the map already."

I shake my head. I don't know.

"We should eat," Hugo says, "and drink."

"Yeah, come on," Dad says. "Let us treat you to dinner. It's the least we can do."

"Well . . ." Aaron smiles not at us but at Liat, I realize. I never asked about Aaron's wife, Hugo's mom. I look around—there are only photos of Hugo and his dad, so she doesn't seem to be in the picture, literally. "Yes, let's go eat. I would love a glass of wine."

Outside, the air is warm, and the sky is tinted ever so slightly orange as the sun drops on the horizon. Aaron and Hugo lead us to a cozy-looking restaurant with a dark red awning. They don't have a table large enough for all seven of us, so we split up by age: Dad, Liat, Sterling, and Aaron at one table; Gabe and me with Hugo at another nearby. We order quickly, Gabe and Hugo translating the menu for me, then drink soda and wait and talk. The restaurant is warm and smells delicious, like butter and thyme.

"I hope my father's English is good enough," Hugo says, looking over at the adults. Dad and Liat are telling some story already, Dad using big hand gestures as Liat rolls her eyes and interrupts.

"I'm sure it'll be fine," I say.

Hugo turns to me, his eyes flicking between Gabe and me as he smiles. "Plus it is nice to have some time with just us, right?" he says.

Gabe squeezes my leg under the table, but I'm not sure what he's trying to say—this is hot? Funny? Both? I think it's kind of both. But also a little weird. Hugo's a fan. He's hitting on me, but I shouldn't, like, flirt with fans, right? Or is that okay? Even maybe to do more than flirt, as long as I'm honest about what's happening and don't make Hugo think it's something it's not?

"So you like Ten's TikTok?" Gabe asks.

"And Instagram," Hugo says. "All the queer kids at my school, we enjoy the history lessons from them."

"Big history fans?" I ask.

"Oh yes, I hope to take my *baccalauréat général* next year so I can one day teach history."

"That's like the SATs," Gabe says.

"I want to use your videos in classes I teach. We don't learn so much of this."

"Not us, either," Gabe says sadly. "Like, some schools have small sections on Stonewall and stuff, but not the big stuff. Not until college—university."

"And they're trying to ban teaching any of it in some places," I say.

"They try to hide these things from us to keep us scared and powerless, right?" Hugo says, quoting one of my videos.

I grin. Okay. That was definitely hot.

"It's the truth," I say. "But I'm glad that people are watching—glad that you want to teach students. I don't think I'd actually be a good teacher."

"What?" Gabe asks, half laughing.

Hugo laughs with him. "That's what your videos are."

"Yeah, but I can't do structure. A syllabus. I would just want to get up there and talk about whatever was interesting me that week."

"Ah, yes," Hugo says. "That might not be best, then. But that is all right. You do your show, your TikToks, and we will make it into a syllabus."

"So do you watch the show?"

Hugo shakes his head, frowning. "It is difficult to stream here."

I nod. Our old seasons were on a smaller channel, and which countries they aired in always felt sort of random. My Greek friend, Leo, thought he'd seen every season, but he'd missed the first one. He said he didn't mind, though, since I wasn't on it.

"Well, the next season I bet will air everywhere, because it's on a huge network," Gabe says. "You'll be able to see it."

Hugo lights up. "I hope so. Papa will be on it."

"And your motorcycle," Gabe says. We laugh, and I try to smile, but this talk of seasons and next season is making me think of my talk with Sterling again. I glance over at her. She's drinking a large glass of red wine, smiling and nodding sometimes. This was a scary day for her. And she stuck by us. She really does care about the show, in her way. Publicity, branding, money . . . I should try not to make her life so hard. But I wish I didn't have to think about any of it. I sort of wish it could be like it was before. But Dad says even that would be hard to get back to.

"So can you give me a preview? What did you find in the house where I met you?"

"Oh, man," Gabe says. "It was insane." I let Gabe tell the story of our escape from the mechanical room as I sip my soda.

"So what was the map of?" Hugo asks.

"France," I say with a sigh. "But . . . there was nothing on it." I take out my phone, bring up the photo, and show it to him. "Liat thinks maybe there were some hidden chemical markings, but . . ." I shrug. "I genuinely don't know what to do next. That's why we're sitting down, eating, relaxing. We need to recharge."

Hugo tilts the photo of the map, squinting at it. "The border reminds me of something."

"It does?" I ask, looking over his shoulder. He blushes but leans into me. I stare at the border with its loops. "I guess . . . the letter, kind of, right?"

"Yes, that's it!" Hugo says. "The letter had a border . . . not quite like this. No loops, but, like . . . um . . . small, the word escapes—triangles?"

"Points, yeah," I say, taking my phone back and flipping to the photos of the letter I'd taken. The spikes of the inked border do look like the loops, somehow, like they fit together. "I wonder if . . ."

I get out my tablet from my backpack and bring the photos up on the bigger screen in an art program.

"The map was a lot bigger, though," Gabe says, looking over my shoulder. Hugo is looking over my other shoulder. The waiter comes with our food, but we ignore it.

"If I arrange the letter so that the points from its border line up with the loops from the map's border . . ." It's not too hard to figure out. Each side has one, two, three, or four loops respectively, so I know how they line up, and then I just move the letter around on the map until it's in place.

"Okay . . . ," I say when it's done. "But what does that do?"

"Tenny?" Dad asks, apparently realizing we're on to something.

"Maybe the accent marks . . ."

"The seal," Liat says, now standing behind me. "That has to be it. The letter's seal marks where to go on the map. Good work."

"So where is it?" I say, looking at my cassoulet and wishing I had time to eat it. But we need to catch up to the men who stole everything. And who knows where the Vatican's goons are? "We should leave."

Hugo pulls out his phone and looks something up. "You can leave, but you will not get there until tomorrow night. So you may as well leave tomorrow morning. It is only about four hours by train."

"What?" I ask, thinking his English is finally failing him.

"It is the Abbaye de Saint-David-la-Roi, on the Monte de Saint-David."

"What?" I repeat.

"Oh," Gabe says. "Yeah, I remember reading about this place. It's an island off the coast, but during certain low tides, the water goes low enough you can walk to it."

"Yes," Hugo says, "and according to their website, the next walkable low tide will not be until just before sunset tomorrow."

"Can't we just take a boat?" Dad asks.

"They didn't build a road?" Liat says at the same time.

"No." Hugo shakes his head. "A road or bridge would interfere with the classical architecture, and no one will pilot a boat there. The water is shallow enough to be dangerous, and it is considered bad luck. You only go to Saint-David-la-Roi when it is open to you. It is a beautiful little city. We went there once. Stone streets, alleys with flowers. Like from another time."

"Did you see a lyre there?" I ask.

Hugo laughs and shakes his head. "I thought it was just a tourist town."

"Of course it would be on an island called Saint David the King," Dad says. "We should have started there."

"We followed the trail," Liat says. "You know how many churches and abbeys named for Saint David there are?"

"So . . . we can get a train tomorrow, I guess," Dad says, sitting back down.

"We can sleep tonight, then?" Sterling asks, hopeful.

"Yeah," Dad says. "Get us some hotel rooms."

"I'll pay you back for mine," Liat says. "Don't want someone thinking we can share." She gives Dad some side-eye, and he grins.

"So we can eat?" I say, finally turning to my food.

"Please?" Gabe asks.

"Yeah," Dad says with a laugh. "I mean, the food is already here."

We all dig in, and the food is delicious and still warm, but my mind is already miles away, waiting for sunset so I can cross an ocean and finally get that lyre.

❧ ELEVEN ❧

Gabe and I order everything off the dessert menu to try and spend almost an hour ranking our favorites with Hugo as Dad and his table share another bottle of wine. I genuinely cannot choose a winner between the flaky galette de rois and buttery tarte tatin, but Gabe and Hugo give it to the galette. It's nice to have a moment to relax. We've been chasing the lyre for just a few days, but it feels like we haven't slowed down. I know we slept in Venice, but that feels like weeks ago already. After the meal, we walk to the hotel, where we all say good night to Aaron, who kisses Liat's hand. Dad, Liat, and Sterling go inside, but Gabe, Hugo, and I linger, taking in the air, which smells like dark chocolate. Aaron tells his son to get home by midnight, then walks off.

"It's so pretty here," Gabe says, looking out at the river Seine, which runs near the hotel.

The sky is dark, but the buildings make stars on the water's surface.

"I don't know if I appreciate it enough sometimes," Hugo says. He's standing close between us.

I look over at Gabe, who wiggles his eyebrows. I know that look.

"You want to see if we have a view from our room?" I ask.

Hugo grins. "Sure."

Upstairs, we spend very little time admiring the river, but the views are incredible anyway.

Hugo leaves a little before midnight after taking one more selfie with Gabe and me. I didn't let him take any pictures of us naked—wouldn't want those getting out—but I don't mind being shirtless so he can brag about it to his friends.

"Was that weird?" Gabe asks, lying across the bedcover. "I mean, not what we did, but that he was a fan, and he, like . . . wanted us because of social media?"

"I think a lot of people meet on social media for sex," I say. "And he wasn't just some random fan by the time we brought him up here. He was fun and smart, and he wants to be a history teacher . . . We had a little date first. And he knew we'd be gone in the morning. We were all on the same page. If he'd just met us outside the mechanical room and then asked if he could come up with us, I'd have said no."

"I might not have," Gabe says with a grin. "He's cute. And that was fun."

"It was," I say, lying down on Gabe's chest. He turns off the lamp, but there's still some light creeping in from the window, turning the room a pale blue. "You think it'll be there?"

"What?" Gabe asks.

"The lyre."

He laughs. "I thought we were still talking threesomes."

I laugh, too. "Yeah, sorry, no, on to the main thing again. Can't you read my mind by now?"

"You know, I kind of can. And I know you're asking because you're worried—about getting to it first, about recovering it, about the show . . . You've been wearing that worry all day."

"Yeah," I say.

"So I don't know if the lyre will be there, or if someone else moved it or got to it first, or any of that. But I know you're doing a genuinely amazing job finding it. Watching you in that room today . . . that was something else, Ten. I mean, I've seen it on TV, but you get so focused, and you're so smart . . . I don't know if the lyre is waiting for us. But I know you've earned it. So it should be."

I pick up Gabe's injured hand. He changed the bandage himself, and maybe overwrapped it, making it seem bulkier.

"So no regrets?" I ask him. "Your parents are going to be so mad at me."

"I'll tell them it was my fault. I slammed it in a door or something."

"Won't they see it on the show?"

He shrugs. "We can edit that part, right?"

I laugh.

"But no, no regrets. It hurts a little, but I can move it fine, and it'll leave a cool scar, like yours." He runs his other hand along the scar on my leg. "This has been the most fun I've had in ages. And now I have a souvenir to remember it by."

I smile and tilt my head so I can kiss his chest.

He laughs. "That tickles."

"Thank you," I say.

"That's what best friends are for," he says. "But I'm gonna fall asleep like any second now."

"Yeah, me too."

The next morning, we buy some pastries and then get on a train to Monte de Saint-David. I feel refreshed after sleeping for eight hours, and the pastries fill me with equally refreshing sugar. Liat talked to the board of the USJHA, and the board members were thrilled by the idea of us teaming up. They happily agreed to my terms about making sure the queer history is highlighted as much as the Jewish history. That fills me up and energizes me, too. If we find the lyre—and we've got to—it'll be like my history is up there, on display. Jewish, queer. Not in conflict, either, just presented as a part of history. Like it is. And like I am, too. Honestly, that's a better feeling than any sugar rush.

We've spread out across the aisle in the train, all of us reading about Monte de Saint-David, the abbey and town on this weird sometimes-island. In the photos it looks beautiful, a spiraling mountain covered with a city. Originally built in the sixth century as a fort because it was so difficult to access, that same natural defense meant people flocked to it over the years to escape the wars that so often plagued the mainland. The walls became more fortified, and the abbey was built, which is when the name changed and a lot more people moved in. It was both a structurally sound little fort that fought off invaders with its natural fortifications and a blissful little town, an escape for so many who had no interest in fighting.

During the Renaissance, the town flourished, becoming a home to several master clock- and toy makers. That makes me raise an eyebrow.

There's no mention of a secret society of David, but the name of the place might make that harder to find among all the David references. I study the photos instead, looking for clues. The buildings have been redone and built up over the years, but it still looks medieval. It looks like something from a museum. I half expect it to be filled with historical reenactors when I get there.

"Hey, so, good news," Sterling says, moving seats to sit across from me. "Thrill loves the idea of a live ad. On your TikTok, they think. They're going to write up a script and send one over, but if you do that and link it to all your other socials, they will give us a significant bonus that we can apply toward PR for the show."

"A script?" I ask.

"Yeah, just, like, 'I love using Thrill products on my adventures because they smell great and work great' but probably better written than that."

I laugh, but it sounds sad. "A talk-to-the-camera moment. Dad selling trail mix."

She shrugs. "I know I said you wouldn't have to, but . . . yeah. For your socials. It will help us a lot, Ten. If you do this and we find the lyre, you'll have a real shot at getting that *Out* cover, getting a second season . . ."

"Okay." I nod. "I'm in."

"Really?"

"Don't question it. You'll make me question it," I say. "But . . . I believe you know what you're doing. So . . . if I have to talk about how great Thrill hand cream is in order to keep doing what I do . . . sure."

She reaches out and squeezes my shoulder. She's beaming. "I'm so glad," she says. "In fact . . . think you might want to use that hand cream now?" She takes out one of the smaller cameras and points it at me.

I roll my eyes but put on some hand cream while gazing out the window. It's a little greasy, but I don't mind. Then I turn and start telling the camera about where we're going, what we've discovered. Sterling keeps filming, which I'm glad about. At least this way the hand cream won't look too forced. Well, yes it will, but at least it won't just be a random shot of me putting on hand cream.

When I'm done and she stops filming, she squeezes my arm affectionately. "I really do love what you do."

"Thanks," I say.

"I also really hope there are no more falling spiked ceilings, though."

"Nah," Dad says from across the aisle. "Maybe spiked floors, though. Where they pop out if you step on the wrong tile or something. Done that one five times."

Liat scoffs next to him. "Six."

"What?" Dad asks. "Where?"

Liat starts listing her spiked-floor encounters, and I turn back to my tablet, looking at photos of Monte de Saint-David, the winding streets, the shops, the many clock towers. There's one large farm where the island gets most of its dairy and vegetables: two fields at the top of the spiral main street that wraps around the abbey. Otherwise, the mont is all cobblestones and high walls.

Gabe sits down next to me and nudges me, showing me his iPhone, where he's pulled up an article about secret tunnels under the island.

"Doesn't say where the entrances are, though," he says, frowning.

I squeeze his leg. "Let's keep an eye on the ground, then. But it could just be someone sensationalizing an old sewer system. They must have one, or else the whole town would turn into a waterslide in the rain."

"That would be cool, though."

"The streets are all cobblestone. I think it would hurt."

He laughs. "Yeah, probably." He leans his head on my shoulder. "You think this is the final stop? Will it really be there?"

I inhale and let it out slowly. "I hope so. I think so. After so many places we've been . . . yeah. But the lyre has changed hands so many times that I don't know. It's possible it'll just be a dead end."

"Oooof." He goes slack, like I hit him.

"But my gut is saying this is it. If I can trust my gut."

"Sure you can," Dad says, turning to me suddenly. "Mine says it, too."

"And mine," Liat adds.

"Adventurer's gut," Dad says.

"Sounds like a stomach virus," I say.

Dad and Liat laugh.

"We'll need to move fast when the train stops," Liat says. "If we're right, we still need to get there first."

❧ TWELVE ❧

When the train stops, we're first in line to get off, and Sterling has already arranged for a van to meet us at the station. The mainland town across from Monte de Saint-David is more modern than the one we're heading for. It's got tall buildings, a few very modern, all glass, and some old stone ones. Traffic lights—hell, traffic. We stop for lunch, but the whole time my leg is shaking. I wish I could make the tide roll out faster. The sun doesn't set until around ten p.m. local time (the French love a late sunset). The path to the mont doesn't clear until ten forty-three. We'll be on the shore, ready to cross, at ten thirty, we decide. So after lunch we get some rooms at a local hotel to rest up for the adventure ahead. We'll have to hit the mont running.

I try to sleep, and do so in fits and starts, dreaming of a lyre at the end of a long hallway I keep running down. When it's time, we all eat in silence, Dad trying to crack a few jokes. But we're all nervous. It electrifies the air between us. Close and waiting is the worst, I decide.

The road to the mont is paved, sort of. Asphalt leads out of the mainland town, down a long road to the beach. The road ends with a gate and a sign saying no vehicles beyond this point. The sun is low enough that it disappears behind the mont, which we can see across the expanse of water. The sea looks so flat, you could walk on it. The shadow of the mont itself reflects in its surface, almost like a dark pit in the water. I take off my shoes and put them in my backpack. Sterling, finally learning, left her camera bag in the hotel and has only the little travel cameras with her. She wears a backpack slung over her shoulders, like the rest of us.

There's a small crowd waiting at the water's edge, watching the sun set behind the silhouette of the mountain town. They're just dark figures, lit the way they are, but as we walk to the front of the crowd, I recognize one: Father Eriksen. He smiles and nods at me, then walks closer. I want to pull back, the way you would from a poisonous snake, but instead I lock eyes with him and keep my face blank.

"Congratulations on making it here," he says. He looks at my father and Liat. "To all of you."

"How'd you make it so far?" Dad asks, balling his hands into fists. "You send that thug to attack my son?"

Eriksen shakes his head, but his expression remains placid. "I don't know what you mean. I used Vatican resources to track the lyre here. I know exactly where I'm going. I don't need to resort to violence."

"No?" Dad asks, looking at the two large men in suits standing behind Eriksen. They aren't the ones who came out of Hugo and Aaron's apartment.

"That's what they're for," Liat says.

"Don't be ridiculous," Eriksen says. "I did historical investigation, same as you must have, I imagine."

"Where did you research?" Dad asks.

"We have an extensive collection in the Vatican," Eriksen says. "If you're willing to give up this search, I'd be happy to show you a few select objects . . ."

"No." It's not me saying it. Not Dad, either. It's not even Gabe or Liat. Sterling. I turn around, shocked. She looks a little shocked, too. "We've come so far. And . . . I'm still not sure I believe the whole David-and-Jonathan-as-lovers thing, but . . . I want to see the lyre. I think we deserve to see it."

Father Eriksen smiles faintly. "Maybe you will, at a Vatican exhibition. And there is no need to believe such outlandish lies about King David. There is no need to pervert our ancestors."

"Really?" Gabe says. "You're not even going to couch it in pretty language? Just going to call us perverts?"

"I do not call *you* perverted, merely your interpretation of historical and religious figures."

"Right." Gabe rolls his eyes.

"Ignore him," Liat says. "He's a little dog yapping. We'll beat him to the lyre and then bring it back."

Eriksen smiles at that, then walks away. I watch him, but he just stares at the water, which has begun to recede, revealing a sandbar, like a path through the water to the island mont. Practically biblical. The whole crowd starts to amble forward. The tide will be low enough to walk for about an hour, and then the water will come back up until just after dawn, when it'll be low enough to walk back, according to a website tracking the tides.

The sand is wet under our feet and sticks between my toes as I try to step lightly and not sink. About halfway there, we pass another group of tourists coming back, who wave at us, happy, having had a good time. We wave back. Gabe asks a girl our age how it was.

"Weird," she says in a Spanish accent. She's walking quickly to catch up with her parents. "But cool, too?"

"Thanks!" Gabe shouts back.

We all arrive at the end of the sandbar at around the same time. It's hard to rush on wet sand, so no one has pulled too far ahead or fallen too far behind. Not even Father Eriksen, sadly.

The sand ends in stone steps flecked with seaweed and worn smooth from being washed by the tide. They become dryer and sharper as we walk up them into the town, and we all pause to put our shoes back on. An archway marks the stair's transition into a cobblestone street, which is lined with vendors and people handing out flyers for hotels, clapping, and welcoming the groups. I smile politely at them as they hold up their wares—small medals of St. David the King, cheeses made here on the mont, key chains, postcards—but we don't browse for souvenirs. The first main street spirals up the mountain, smaller alleys and roads branching off it. Every house looks like something from a fairy tale, but for some reason, maybe the setting sun, it's all sinister. Awnings cast windows in darkness. The little alleyways are filled with shadows. Something about this place feels like it's hiding things. I know it is.

Father Eriksen and his henchmen follow the main street forward, ignoring us. Liat nods in their direction. "Should we follow them?"

"Cheating again?" Dad asks.

"They clearly know something. Why not see what it is?"

"I think we should look for the signs of the secret society of David," I say. "The five stones symbol. That's what's going to guide us."

"But maybe Father Eriksen knows where it is already," she says.

I look at Gabe, who shrugs. I'm not sure what to do.

1. Follow Eriksen. He might know exactly where the lyre is, in which case following him still means he'll beat us there. Maybe we can rush ahead and grab it just before he does?

2. It could be a trap. Or Eriksen could have an idea of where to look for clues, in which case our exploring might turn up the lyre faster.

3. Just ignore Eriksen and hope he doesn't waltz out of here with the lyre before we can even find it.

4. There are five of us . . .

"Let's split up," I say.

Dad frowns. "No, no, we never do that. That's how you die."

"We're not in a trap-filled dungeon," I say. "And there's more than just the two of us."

"Look around, Tenny," Dad says. "This whole town could be a trap-filled dungeon. Don't let the cute little balconies and flowerpots fool you. We are on a mountain filled with secrets and dangerous people, and in less than an hour, there will be no way off. Splitting up is a bad idea."

"I can go alone," Liat volunteers. "I'll trail Father Eriksen. You and I can keep in contact with our phones."

"No," Dad says. "Liat, you definitely can't go alone."

She sighs and folds her arms. She's wearing black shorts and a light blue tank top, but when she leans back into the wall, shadows cover everything but her feet. "I agreed we'd work together, not that you'd be the boss."

"Tenny is the boss," Dad says.

"And he's saying we should split up. It'll be fine. I'll go alone. You all stay together." She looks at me, and I nod. She pushes herself off the wall and starts walking after Eriksen. "I'll be in touch," she whispers at us. Dad watches her go, his face switching between anger and fear. He turns back to me finally.

"I wish you hadn't said that," he says, his voice hot.

"It makes the most sense," I say. "We need to get to the lyre before them, or else we lose the queer history and we lose the show. She knows that, and . . . Are you worried she'll back out, take the lyre for herself?"

"What?" He looks offended. "No, of course not. I just . . . It's dangerous."

"But she's capable, right? She's almost as good as you, you said."

"Yeah." He sighs. "Still . . ." He looks over to the shadows that Liat has vanished into. She's gone now. "Let's find something fast so she has to come back and meet us," he says.

"Okay." I nod and pull up a map of the town on my phone, holding it out for Sterling to film. "Gabe found an article about secret tunnels under the island. If that's true, then I think the entrances could have to be higher up, maybe around here, the middle part of the mountain. Any lower, and they'd be underwater. But higher, and they'd be right under the abbey."

"So what are we looking for?" Gabe asks.

"The symbol," I say again. "The five stones. Maybe the virtues written in French or . . . anything else. Anything related to David."

"That's going to be a lot here," Dad says. He points at a sign for a souvenir shop:

Mont de Saint-David-le-Roi Souvenirs

"Yeah," I say. "And I guess anything with lyres or Jonathan." Maybe there's some secret queer code. Probably not; the secret society of David definitely didn't seem to feel that David and Jonathan were more than just "good friends." Trying to find their hiding place with my mentality will be pointless. Still, a part of me hopes.

We start walking up the main street. It's getting darker and darker, the sky turning purple, then navy. The air smells strongly of the ocean, salty and strong, but also of something baking, cigarette smoke. It's not cold, exactly—it's still summer—but the breeze is strong and makes my skin prickle with goose bumps. Around us, most shops are closed aside from a few restaurants and bars. From those, we can hear noisy laughter in bursts as doors open, sudden shots of sound in the quiet. Otherwise, all we can hear are our footsteps and the waves that surround us, growing higher.

I scan the walls for anything that could be a clue. As Dad said, there are depictions of David everywhere. Many are variations on Michelangelo's famous statue of David naked and young, holding his sling. David on hotel windows, David painted on the walls, small statues of David lined up in shop windows, price tags covering his junk: only €14.99. It almost makes me smile, and I take out my own camera to film, narrating over it.

"All these little souvenirs, these signs and images . . . all celebrating a queer man. That's . . . kind of cool. Even if they don't know it."

Gabe grins when he hears me and stops to point at the row of Davids in the window. "I'll buy you one tomorrow."

"I'll buy *you* one," I respond, grinning. "We can have a pair."

"What about this?" Sterling asks suddenly, pointing at the corner of a building, where the words RUE DU FOI have been carved.

"We're on Faith Street," Gabe says, looking down the narrow alley. "Should we check it out?"

We're not quite halfway up the mont yet, but I nod—it's worth investigating. The alley isn't well lit, and all but one of the windows that look out onto it are closed. The one open window has translucent shades drawn and casts a square of hazy yellow light on the left wall of the alley. I take out my phone and use it as a flashlight, surveying the walls up and down for any sign of anything.

"There's a sewer drain," Gabe says, pointing his light at a small drain at the edge of a building. "You said there must be an old sewer system, right?"

"Yeah."

"And that maybe that's what the secret tunnels are?"

"Maybe," I say. "But we can't get in through this one." I kneel and shine my flashlight inside. It's just darkness leading down.

"Are we going to have to wade in the sewers?" Sterling asks with a sigh.

I shrug and keep looking at the walls. There's nothing, though. I take out the map again and see if there are any other streets named for the five virtues, but Rue du Foi is the only one. And there's nothing here.

Dad's phone beeps, and he takes it out. "Liat."

"What's she saying?" I ask, walking up to him and looking over his shoulder.

The . . . is blinking, and then the message comes in:

LIAT

The guy who stole the map is here

LIAT

They're meeting with him outside the abbey

LIAT

He's giving Eriksen something

"The map and the letter?" I ask. "But if Eriksen didn't have those, how did he know to come here?"

HENRY

The map?

LIAT

I don't know

LIAT

The guy left, Eriksen going into abbey with his men

LIAT

I'm following

"So the Vatican paid someone to steal the map," Dad says.

"Should we go follow them, then?" Gabe asks. "They clearly know stuff we don't."

I shake my head. "No, we'll stay here. Liat is following them. If we don't find anything else, we can meet them at the abbey, maybe . . . I don't know."

"Take the lyre?" Gabe asks. He sounds uncertain. So am I. Finding the lyre is one thing. Stealing it from a priest with hired muscle is another. That's why we have to find another way.

Dad types into his phone.

HENRY

Be careful

LIAT

"She okay?" Gabe asks.

"I hope so," I say. "If it's too dangerous, we can tell her to come back. We can all regroup and plan—"

"She wouldn't," Dad says. "Best we can do is find some clue to the lyre. Then she'll come back and meet us. We need to keep looking."

"Okay, so this is the only street in town named for one of the virtues," I say, "and it's a dead end. So do we just keep looking around, head up to the middle of the island like I suggested?"

"*Foi*," Dad says. "Faith. I feel like it's a clue. David showed faith by not wearing the fancy armor King Saul offered him, right?"

"Yeah," I say, looking back down the alley. There are no signs, no five little circles to represent the society, but faith would mean . . . believing in something even if it isn't there—protection, even if you have no armor. I pull up the map on my phone again and look at it. On the other side of this dead end is another dead end; a cute little house with an orange steepled roof is in the middle of what could have been a street. Maybe it was once. There's a window on the second floor, brown painted wood with shutters closed, and below it is a wall of stones. I walk up to the wall and run my hands over the stones. They're not carved to be identical—none of these buildings are made from anything like that. They're too old. These are rocks of different sizes, colors, all worn smooth by years of salt air.

"Tenny?"

I run my hand up and down the wall, feeling for something, anything.

One rock shakes ever so slightly. Faith. I push the rock in, and there's the faintest click.

"What was that?" Sterling asks.

The one that clicked was small, to the left of the wall. I run my hand over to the right, find another one like it, and push it in. Another click. There'll be three more, I know, all laid out like the five stones of the society's symbol. There but unseen. You need to have faith to find them.

I turn around to make sure Sterling is filming, then quietly explain my thinking as I find the last three stones and push on each. "Faith Street. Faith is believing in something—God's protection—even when you have no evidence." *Click.* Two left. "Something there that isn't. So they hid something here: their symbol." *Click.* One left. I trace my hand to where the last stone should be and push. This click is louder. The whole wall rumbles and then slowly swings inward on invisible seams between the stones. A door.

"Nice work, Tenny," Dad says, already going through the opening in the wall.

"That was hot," Gabe says, his hand on the small of my back and drifting lower.

"Thanks," I say. "I wasn't sure it would work."

"What's inside?" Sterling asks, peeking into the darkness Dad just went through.

"Lotta spiderwebs," Dad calls out. "And a passage. Come on."

I'm about to follow Dad when I look down and see a small polished stone, about the size of a tennis ball, perfectly round. It was waiting right in the middle of where the doorway opened, like it's important. I pick it up. It doesn't rattle or feel special. Just a carved rock sphere. Still, I put it in my bag. Then I walk into the secret passage, my phone held high as a flashlight. Dad was right; there are a lot of spiderwebs. Otherwise it's just a stone corridor. It slants slightly and curves, like a spiral heading down.

"Text Liat," I remind Dad. "Tell her we found something."

"I am," Dad says as we walk farther down the hall. It's looping down, I realize, like a spiral staircase. We walk a few minutes more before it flattens out again. We're now in a small circular room with a door on the far end. I approach and shine my phone on it. Thick wood. I push, but it doesn't give.

"Look," Gabe says, shining his phone light a little higher. The word *autorité* is carved into the door.

"I'm getting so sick of these five words," I say with a sigh.

"Here's a shepherd's crook," Dad says, finding one leaning against the wall near the door. "Maybe it's the key?" He tries lifting it. "It's metal," he says, confused. "Heavy."

"There are balls around the room," Gabe says, pointing. I approach. They're also metal, black, a little bigger than tennis balls. I try lifting one, but it is either too heavy or stuck to the wall somehow.

"And there's a hole in the door," Sterling says, pointing as she films, the light from her camera illuminating the floor better. A small carved hole sits in the bottom of the door, like a mousehole. I get down to look at it. It doesn't go all the way through the door—it curves down into a hole in the floor.

"Okay . . . ," I say. "There's a hole . . . maybe for the balls to go down there. But the balls don't move, unless . . ." I roll my eyes and go over to the shepherd's crook. It's heavy, but not as heavy as the balls. I can lift it. I bring it over to one of the balls, and sure enough, the staff's tip rolls it. I can feel the force of it—magnets. "Really?" I ask. "This isn't so much a riddle as just annoying."

Gabe chuckles, and Sterling films me as I try to herd all the balls into the hole in the door. The crook is magnetized on both ends, and the orbs seem to have different magnetic polarities, so sometimes the crook will move one orb one way but another in a different direction. I try to focus on one at a time, slowly herding each ball into the hole, where it falls with a satisfying *plunk*.

"I guess, for leadership, they just wanted you to prove that you can get something done."

"Taking charge, menial tasks. Maybe this is humility, too," I say. "Would be nice to not have to go through all five."

When the final orb goes into the hole, the door creaks open. Dad looks at his phone.

"Liat hasn't answered."

"You think she's in trouble?" I ask. "Should we go back?"

"She'd kill me if I went back," Dad says, shaking his head. "No, no, just . . . let's be careful."

In the center of floor of the hallway that opens in front of us is another round stone. I pick it up.

"What's that?" Dad asks.

"Just a carved stone. Smooth, nothing on it," I say. "But there was one at the first door, too, so . . ." I put this one in my bag, too.

Dad nods. "Good call. Let's keep moving forward for now, though."

The hall slopes and turns again, another spiral downward, and at the end of it, another small circular room and another door. *Humilité.*

"I really half hoped we'd just finished this puzzle," I say, looking around the room. There are shelves, and the shelves are covered in keys. Large and ornate, small and expensive—keys everywhere.

"I think I've seen this one," Gabe says. "The humblest key?"

"Probably," I say. "These barely feel like tests, honestly."

"I don't know if they are," Dad says as we all survey the keys. "There's no danger. I don't think we'll lose anything but time if we pick the wrong key . . . I think these are rituals."

"Rituals?" Gabe asks. "Like . . . to summon something?"

"No, no," Dad says. "Well . . . who knows? But these chivalric orders, they were very ritualized, and often when a novice joined, they'd have to perform some ritual. Usually nothing life-threatening. Maybe kill a pig or something. There were genuinely occult orders, of course. In those maybe you had to kill a virgin, but there was still no mortal danger for the initiate."

"So you think we found an initiation entrance?" I ask.

Dad nods.

"But there's another?"

"Probably for the folks already initiated. No one would want to do all these little chores every time they entered the . . . sanctum? Clubhouse? Ah!" He holds up a simple bronze key. "Humble enough?" He walks over to the door.

"But if Father Eriksen knows the door for the already initiated . . . ," I say as Dad puts the key in the lock and turns it.

"Yeah," he says, pulling open the door. "They'll get there a lot quicker."

"We need to hurry," I say, racing ahead. There's another round stone on the floor, but Dad pockets this one, all of us eager to move forward. The hall slants and curves again, down to the next ritual room.

"I don't have a signal," Dad says as we walk. "And Liat never texted back."

"If she's still tailing Eriksen, maybe she'll find her own way down," I say.

"I hope . . . ," Dad says.

I shine my flashlight on the next room. In the center of it is a fountain that's still working, depicting life-size naked women bathing, each holding a seashell. The water pours down around them. I go over to examine it—there's only a little moss, no rust, on the fountain.

"Someone has been maintaining this," I say.

"Like . . . the society?" Gabe asks. "You think they're still . . . around?"

"Maybe?" I say, though it sounds unlikely. I look over at the door, shine my light on it.

Unsurprisingly, it says *virilité*.

"So we're supposed to pick the most . . . fertile?" Gabe asks.

"Could be," I say. "Bathsheba's first kid by David died after childbirth—struck down for his infidelity—but then they had a whole lot more. But this is more about David's fertility than hers, right? So maybe . . . the most alluring?"

"This one," Dad says, pointing at one of the statues with a grin that makes me frown.

"Dad, gross."

"Look, all women are beautiful," he says, winking at the camera. Sterling scoffs. "But it's this one."

"The shells probably mean something," I say.

"It's this one," Dad says, still staring at the woman. She's holding what looks like a unicorn horn.

"I don't know anything about shells, though." I look at Gabe, but he shakes his head.

"I . . . do," Sterling says after a moment.

"You do?" I ask, surprised. It's hard to imagine her knowing anything about anything besides social media engagement and advertiser metrics.

"I collect them," she says, hunching her shoulders in a shrug that stays up with embarrassment. "Summers growing up, we'd go to the beach every weekend, and I'd pick them up, and it became sort of a thing, so I read all about them, and . . ."

I smile.

"I get it, it's silly," she says.

"No, no," I say quickly. "Just nice to hear you talk about something besides advertising."

"Well, I am a person," she says, frowning. "I have interests."

"Shells," Gabe says.

"Yes." She glances away—I think she's blushing—then looks over at the fountain and approaches it. "Oyster, scallop, conch, nautilus, and auger," she says, pointing out each one and ending on the shell Dad has proclaimed is his favorite. "They all represent ideas of fertility. Well, sort of. Like, the scallop is actually associated with the Virgin Mary during the Renaissance, but the *Venus Rising* painting took that and made it sexy, so there's some fertility stuff there. The conch was strength, or sometimes just the luxury of owning an expensive shell. Coorte painted all these shells. I went to an exhibit."

"Wow," I say, impressed. "You really like shells."

"They're neat," she says, smiling. "The nautilus symbolized beauty and knowledge . . . so that one I think you can cross off. Then there's the oyster and the auger. Those are definitely fertility. The auger is . . . sort of virility, for obvious reasons." She points at the way the statue is holding the unicorn-horn shell. "And the oyster is fertility."

"Okay, so let's think like this society, then," I say, looking between the two shells. "One is clearly more . . . masculine."

"Yeah, the right one," Dad says.

"I mean . . . if it's about David's fertility, not Bathsheba's . . . ," Gabe says, looking at Dad's choice.

"Yeah." I sigh. "It makes sense."

"Told ya," Dad says, reaching out and grabbing the shell the woman is holding. He twists it, and there's a click from the door. "Never doubt my taste in women."

"All of them?" I ask.

Dad laughs. "Come on. Four down. One more and maybe we'll get to the lyre before Eriksen."

That makes my pulse rise again. If Eriksen has the easy way in, I don't know how we can beat them to the lyre at this point. But maybe there are more locks to get through.

Another round stone—this time Gabe picks it up—and another hall that tilts down and spirals, leading to another circular room. *Fraternité* is stamped on the door, but I don't see anything else.

"What do we do?" I ask.

Gabe pushes on the door, but it's locked.

"There's a floor plate here," Dad says, shining his light in the center of the room. It's slightly raised. "Maybe we just step on it?"

He puts his foot down. There's a click, but when we try the door, it's still locked.

"Okay," I say. "Fraternity, Jonathan. The box and the mechanical room both showed the scene where he strips as representative of his and David's relationship."

Gabe snorts. "Very straight."

"So . . ." I feel the laugh start in my throat. "I think you gotta strip, Dad."

"What?" Dad says. "Why me?"

"You're on the plate. It's weighing you. So now the door will probably open when you get lighter by removing the weight of your clothes."

"Oh." Dad grins. "Sure. But you mean the weight of *their* clothes." He shrugs off his backpack. "Which I'm guessing were just robes." He puts his backpack down on the ground. The door creaks again, and I push it open. Dad turns to the camera. "Sorry, viewers. No nudity this time."

We all roll our eyes.

"Come on," I say, waving everyone to the door. There's a stone sphere just beyond it, and I pick it up. "We're almost there."

❦ THIRTEEN ❦

Through the door are stairs going down, and we follow them. As we walk, I start to hear something.

"Waves," Gabe says.

"And it smells like salt," Dad adds. "We must be at the very bottom of the mont. And with the tide coming back in . . . be careful. Everyone can swim, right?"

"Yeah," Gabe says.

"Sterling, switch out your SD card and make sure everything is waterproofed, and be sure to use the waterproof camera. We once lost some footage to a water trap."

"Okay," Sterling says. "Give me a sec."

I walk slowly, waiting for her to change everything out. The stairs just keep going for a while, but then we can hear something over the waves. Voices.

"We have kept this safe for centuries," says a low male voice with a French accent.

"And now *we* will," says another voice. Eriksen. Damn.

"This is a big request," the first voice says.

"We've been over this on the phone. You said if they made it out of your trap, then you'd move it. They did. We got their map."

"So how did they end up here anyway?"

I smile. Sterling has caught up to us by now, and we're all walking as quietly as we can. The stairs end at a closed door. I put my ear against it to hear better.

"I don't know how they ended up here, but if you don't hand over the lyre soon, they'll claim it," Eriksen says.

"If I hand it over, the society is done."

"But imagine that pervert teenager finding it, putting it on TV, using it to groom more young people. You don't want that."

"I will keep it from him."

Eriksen huffs. He sounds angry. "But we agreed—"

"I've changed my mind."

I hear Eriksen sigh and then someone snapping their fingers. Then there's the sound of the Frenchman trying to call out, but he sounds muffled somehow. I crack the door open slightly.

"Careful," Dad whispers.

I'm peering into a huge room—well, not a room exactly. A room would have a floor.

We're at the very bottom of the island, just above sea level. Walls curve around the room like the inside of a tower, the material a mix of carved stone and natural rock. Light comes in from overhead, some skylight I can't make out. Instead of a solid floor, we're standing on a large stone bridge built over the water, one wide enough for a car. The bridge stretches from this door to another door at the other side of the vast space. It crosses a second bridge in the center, forming an *X*.

Under the bridges is the ocean, churning. Someone carved all this out of the base of the island.

I can't see the other two ends, where the second bridge goes, but standing where the bridges meet are Eriksen and his two goons. One of the goons is holding a strange man from behind, arm around his neck. The stranger is gasping, clawing at the goon's arm, soft gurgles just barely audible over the sound of the ocean beneath them.

"May God have mercy on your soul," Eriksen says to the man as he struggles. The goon jerks his arm violently. A small *snap* echoes through the room. The man slumps in his arms. Eriksen gestures, and the goon tosses the body over the edge, where it hits the water with a splash.

"God forgives you. You were righteous," Eriksen tells the goon.

"Long as the money's good," the goon responds.

Eriksen snorts and walks forward. I still can't see the ends of the second bridge. Just down this one bridge to the other door . . . which I realize has opened slightly. Liat's eyes meet mine, and she blows me a silent kiss.

"Liat's here," I whisper to my dad.

He sighs, relieved. "She okay?"

"She's in another stairwell, hiding like us."

I peek my head out farther, trying to see where Eriksen went. The other line of the X-shaped bridge extends to the back of the room, where it becomes a staircase, curving upward along the inside of this tower. But Eriksen isn't on it. I look the other way. The rest of the bridge ends in a large square platform, and in the center of it, within a domed glass case, is what looks like a small wooden lyre.

"I see the lyre," I whisper to everyone.

Under all that is the ocean, swelling and smelling of salt and fish. I look at the water. It's rising. In a few minutes, it'll be higher than the bridges.

Eriksen and his henchmen are quickly approaching the lyre. I'm not sure if we can take them, even if we do have greater numbers. They're clearly trained killers. So I hold back, watching. Eriksen reaches the platform with the glass dome. The case looks about as tall as Eriksen and extends upward from the floor, thin and with no sharp edges, like a long bubble. It looks like there might be something etched in the glass, but I can't see what. Carefully, I sneak through the doorway, staying low, watching.

The platform around the lyre is carved, I can see now. Carved in a way that I would walk more carefully on. Carved in a way Eriksen and his men are ignoring.

There's a sudden *snap* as they step a few strides onto the platform. I watch as metal claws seem to shoot up around them. One of the henchmen is impaled, his white shirt turning red where the sharp metal has shot through him. He stares at the hole in his chest silently, his eyes wide, then empty.

"What?" Eriksen shouts, not sure what's happening. I feel my heart start to beat fast, my blood rushing. Someone else just died. Two in less than a minute.

Eriksen and the other goon are trapped inside a cage formed by the metal claws that killed the first goon. It's all happened so quickly that the arc of blood is just now hitting the ground. Thin metal bars surround them, curved and sharp, creating a roof to the cage.

"What is this?" the other goon asks, sounding scared.

"A trap," Eriksen says. "Quickly, break it down."

The goon tries to bend the bars but can't. "Poor Jimmy," he says.

"Forget Jimmy," Eriksen says. "Think about us."

"Yeah," Liat says, stepping through her door. "The water is rising. The tide is coming back in. You'll drown in there."

I stand up. No point hiding if Liat isn't. Dad, Gabe, and Sterling follow. The door closes behind them. I see Liat's has closed, too.

"Try the door," I tell Gabe. He goes to open it, but it won't budge.

"They set off more than just that trap I think," I say. "We need to get out of here before the tide comes in, too."

"But let's get the lyre first," Dad says.

We approach the platform, and now I can see the carvings more clearly. Tiles depict various stories of David. None look inaccurate. But not all of them are about the five virtues the society worshipped in particular, the ones I've memorized now—the ones Eriksen, who hasn't done any of these tests and rituals, ignored.

"Let us out of here," Eriksen says. His face is red.

"I don't know if we can," Liat says.

"Then go for help," Eriksen says.

"I don't know if there's time," Dad says. "But after we get the lyre, we will."

"No," Eriksen says, reaching out through the bars. "I'll kill you before I let you pervert God's message."

"How?" I ask. "You're in a cage."

Eriksen glowers, furious. He turns on his remaining goon. "Get us out of here and kill them."

The goon starts trying to bend the bars again, but they don't budge. I study the floor. Five specific scenes: shepherding, Goliath, Bathsheba, Jonathan, and playing the lyre. The tiles are big, a few feet by a few feet, but they're not all neatly lined up. I step on the shepherding tile first.

"Careful, Tenny," Dad says.

"I will be," I say, eyeing Eriksen. He's closed his eyes and is praying, but the henchman is looking at me, furious. Behind him, his impaled coworker is bleeding onto the floor. His eyes are open and blank. I look away.

The next tile is Goliath, which takes me within swiping distance of the cage. I hop to it, and suddenly the henchman reaches out, trying to grab me.

"Let us out of here!" he yells. I manage to dodge him by standing on the far end of the tile. I frantically search out the next tile as I can feel his fingers almost touching my throat. "Tenny . . . ," Dad says, sounding scared.

Bathsheba is another hop away, so I leap, trying to get out of range of the henchman's grasp, but I do so too fast. I just barely land on the edge of the Bathsheba tile, and for a moment, I lose my balance, my arms spiraling.

"Ten!" Gabe shouts.

"Punish him," I hear Eriksen whisper.

I lean forward, letting myself fall entirely onto the Bathsheba tile. My knees bang into it with a thud, and my palms scrape on the carved surface, but none of me falls beyond the tile. I take a deep breath.

"Not to alarm anyone, but the water is rising quickly," Liat says.

"Start looking for a way out," I say. "I'll get the lyre."

"We can just leave it," Dad says. "Come back when the water is low again."

I shake my head. "We're almost there."

And we are. It's a short hop to the Jonathan tile, and then one step over to the lyre tile, and then I'm standing in front of the glass dome, the lyre just inside. It's simpler than I thought it would be. Wood, a little gilding, some carvings I can't make out through the glass, but there it is. Finally. I take a breath and can almost smell it through the glass, over the ocean. I can almost feel it, smooth wood in my hand. Here it is. Proof. Proof that these two men loved each other. No matter what the rest of the world thinks.

I look around the dome for some sort of way to raise it, but it's too heavy. There's no latch or door I can find, either. This must have stood up to thousands of rising tides, the lyre still safe inside. It's airtight. But then how do I open it?

"Do I just break it?" I ask, feeling the surface of the glass. It's thick glass, hazy and scratched, probably from the tides, but there's still some faint etching in it that hasn't been worn away yet.

"I don't know. That might trigger a trap," Dad says.

"These stairs lead up," Gabe calls from the other end of the bridge. "But I don't know how far up."

I feel the glass again. The faint etching seems to have a pattern, but it's too faint to see now. I take out the camera to film it as I inspect.

"There's something on the glass," I say. "Some kind of pattern or writing, but it's too worn to make out."

"Can you fill it with something? Dirt? That'll make it stand out more," Dad calls.

I look around. The tiles are salt-stained, no dirt or anything I can see to fill in the grooves. But . . . I almost laugh. I do have something. I take the Thrill hand cream out of my bag and squeeze the tube of it all over the glass dome, wiping it so that it fills the etching but sweeps off the rest of the surface.

It works, too. The hand cream highlights the pattern in white, making it clear: small circles, lines connecting some of them, are placed haphazardly around the entire dome. It's not a pattern I've seen anywhere else.

What is it? There's no David, no clockwork, none of the five virtues. Except . . . five. I carefully look at each of the circles, the way they relate to each other, until I see it: five circles in the same formation as the seal.

"Tenny?" Dad shouts. I look up. They're all waiting by the stairs. The water is high enough that it's level with the bridge. It'll be up to my shoes in just a moment.

"Almost!" I shout back. Then I press down on the five circles, one at a time. Nothing. I push between them. Nothing. I try putting my fingers each on one circle and pressing, and finally, I hear something give. A hiss. And it smells like stale air. A circle in the glass above my hand pops out slightly, then tumbles down, hitting the ground by my feet with a small splash.

I look down. Water has overtaken the bridge now, like a thin puddle under my feet. And the glass dome is lowering into it. The hole in the glass is still too high for me to grab the lyre. It's lowering at the same pace the water is rising. But I almost have it. I reach into my backpack and get out a padded waterproof envelope and then a

216

plastic bag to go around that. When the water is past the soles of my shoes, the lyre is in reach, and I grab it. It's just light wood, so simple. No gems, ivory, nor gold. The strings are somehow still intact, too. And it rattles slightly. I wish I had time to examine it now, but I don't. I put it in the envelope, then in the plastic bag, protecting it from the water.

Then I run for the staircase where everyone is waiting, being careful to step on only the right tiles again.

In the cage, Eriksen is still praying, and his henchman is sitting down, the water rising around him. He looks at me once, his expression sad, then looks away.

"Sorry," I say. "I'll try to send help, if I can."

He doesn't say anything back, so I keep running. The water is high enough that my socks are wet when I reach the staircase. Everyone else is already climbing it, but slowly, looking back for me.

"You got it," Dad says as we race up the stairs. His voice sings with pride.

"Yeah," I say.

"We'll examine it when we're out of here," Liat says.

The stairs are pretty solid, built jutting out of the wall, but open otherwise, with no banister, which makes it pretty dangerous the higher we get. But we manage to climb faster than the water can rise, and I feel a certain relief flooding through me as we do. We got it. We have the lyre! I'm holding queer history. Well . . . if I can get it out of here, anyway. And if we can get out of here, then I can show it to the world—as queer history. We have to get out and keep the lyre undamaged. We have to.

"Wait," Liat says. She's been leading, with Sterling behind her, filming, then Gabe, then Dad, then me. We've just walked by the skylights—fogged glass circles built into the walls at an angle that cast down light. Above us, it's darker.

"What is it?" Dad asks.

"The stairs end," she says. We all carefully walk up to join her. She's right: the stairs end in a small platform that juts out of the wall like the stairs. But there's no door or other entrance.

I start feeling the wall we're up against for a switch or a hidden door, but there's nothing. Below us, the water is rising pretty quickly.

"Should the water even come this high?" Sterling asks.

"We're essentially in a tube deep under the mountain," Liat says. "The dead guy was talking about it as he led Father Eriksen down here. It fills up with the tide, higher than the surface of the ocean outside. I don't know how high, but it sounded pretty high."

"Maybe not," Gabe says, pointing at the wall opposite us. There's a large hole in the wall there, weirdly framed by a carved face, and there's a line on the stone, salt, like the water has never gone higher. Looking closer, I can see it's not really a hole, it's a sluice. It just looks like it's never been closed.

"Okay." Liat nods. "But then we still have another problem: How do we get out?"

"We can wait," Dad says. "The water will go back down. We'll just go back out the way we came."

"*If* the doors have opened," Liat says. "They were tight when we tried to leave. When Father Eriksen set off that trap, I think he locked us all in . . ." Her eyes drift down to the water churning under us, and mine do, too. Eriksen is dead now. Drowned. I sit down on the edge of the platform we're on, my feet dangling. It's not that I've never seen someone die—I had that unfortunate experience a few months ago, while hunting the rings. That man died much more horrifically than this. It's not that I think Eriksen or his men were good people and, with them gone, we've lost some vital part of humanity. But there's something so chilling about this. The quiet way they went as we were dashing upstairs, held underwater until they died. There wasn't anything we could do.

We're stuck here. But it's still . . . haunting.

Gabe sits down next to me. Everyone is quiet. The water reaches the hole in the wall and starts pouring away. It's also covered the skylights, making everything darker. Light from under the water shines up, but it's dim, shimmering and making a kaleidoscope effect on the walls.

"Maybe that's the way out," Gabe says, nodding at the hole the water is pouring through. It is big enough for a person.

"It probably takes us out to the ocean," I say. "We'd have to swim back around to the entrance to the island . . . but maybe."

"That's if it doesn't get narrower as it goes along," Dad says. "If it even leads to the ocean. If it doesn't end up totally flooded so you drown as it carries you . . . No. Way too risky. There's a staircase here. There's a way out. We just have to find it."

The water is bubbling wildly just below my feet. White froth churns up as it runs out of the stairwell through the hole at the same rate as it rises. It's not just the tide, that's for sure. There's some kind of mechanism to keep the water flowing in here.

"If that closed," I say, pointing at the sluice the water is rushing through, "the water would rise, right?"

"Looks that way," Dad says. "You want to ride it up?"

"Up to where?" Liat asks. She looks up, but the area above us is all in shadow. "What if there's just a roof and we drown?"

"Then why are there stairs?" Dad asks. "There must be some reason."

I look everything over again—the platform, the walls, the sluice that the water is running through. It's got a border of carved stone that looks sort of like a face. In fact, it looks exactly like a face—a wide cartoonish one, the gate its mouth. And its eyes are glaring. Just between them is a small circle. It's faint, but it's there, like a target.

"Wait," I say, going into my backpack and taking out one of the stones we found behind every door of the ritual entrance. "If there was a ritual way to get in, then there should be a ritual way to get out, right? After society members completed the tasks and were initiated, they didn't just leave through the other staircase where Liat came in. They probably had an exit. Something celebratory . . ."

"You think this is it?" Dad asks. "So where's the exit?"

"I think there's one more test." I point at the face around the sluice gate and then toss and catch the spherical stone. "Five virtues, five stones, five chances to be like David."

"And knock out Goliath?" Liat says, grinning. "Okay, so we throw the stone, hit him between the eyes . . . What happens?"

I shrug. "Only one way to find out."

I fish the rest of the stones out of my bag, and Dad and Gabe take out the ones they picked up. I distribute them—there are five of us, so we each get one.

"Oh no," Sterling says. "Not me. I'm bad at sports."

"Sterling," I say, "take the stone. You can't just be sitting on the outside telling me to be less gay—"

"I don't—"

"You do, in your way. And I get that you have all this stuff to worry about—the money, the marketing—but doesn't that make you angry? You say you're a fan, so don't you just wish we could make this show and that the network and the sponsors would support it in the way they should?"

"I . . ." She looks down at the stone I'm offering her. "Yes. I do. But that's not how the world works."

"I know," I say. "I'm queer. And usually this show is my happy place, but you've sort of . . . brought in all the straight stuff. The bad comments that I try to ignore. And that's not your fault. But I'd feel a lot better if, instead of just telling me all that stuff, I knew how angry you were about it. If I knew you hated it, too."

"I do," she says. "I'm sorry if I haven't said that. But I do hate it."

"Good. Then take this stone and channel all that anger into throwing it at the target. There are five of us and five stones. We're all in this together, okay?"

"Okay," she says, taking the stone and handing the camera to Dad. She stares down at the rock and her hand tightens around it. Her whole expression clenches, too, her frown almost swallowing up her face, and then she looks up and hurls the stone. It flies forward and hits Goliath's face. But not the target. She hit his eye.

She sighs. "I told you."

"It was a good try," I say.

Dad tries next, his rock hitting only a little closer than Sterling's. "I never did baseball," he says with a shrug.

"Please," Liat says. "You never did any sports. You were studying in the library your whole youth."

"I played golf," Dad says. "Once."

I laugh. Liat steps up next and throws her stone. It hits just above the target. I'm starting to feel nervous now. I thought for sure she or Dad would hit the open mouth. What happens if we all miss? I guess we have other things in the bag we can throw at it: tubes of Thrill, our shoes . . .

Gabe runs forward and throws his rock with a grunt, but it goes wide, hitting Goliath's ear. He grimaces. "Sorry."

This means it's down to me. I really want to hand my sphere to Dad, but after that speech to Sterling, I know I can't. She's got the camera pointed at me. So I think about David. Not the stupid David whom the secret society believed in, with his five virtues, but the real David I know from my studies. A musician who was launched to fame for one throw of a stone and who fell in love with the king's son and then, when the king tried to separate them, tried to become king himself. Did David do it for Jonathan? Did he think Jonathan would choose him over his father? Did David do it so that he would be remembered? All that riding on one throw of the stone. If he hadn't killed Goliath, would anyone ever have remembered him? Would he ever have been able to tell his own story?

I want to tell my story. That's what I've learned from Sterling. That letting someone else control your story is like letting historians turn you straight. When she first appeared, I thought it was like my history was being erased, and it was, but I've fought back best I could, with my replies on social media and with the story this season will tell. With this lyre. I don't know what people will say about me in the future, after the show airs, but I've tried to be myself, haven't I?

If I'm going to be remembered, that's how I want to be remembered. As myself.

That's what David would have wanted, too. Not the way the secret society looks at him, or the Vatican, or even Sterling. He would want to be remembered for who he was—and that includes being queer.

With all that in me, I throw the stone, hoping that, like David, this one rock can somehow preserve my memory.

❦ FOURTEEN ❦

The rock soars forward, almost in slow motion. The water under us churns, loud. The stone hits Goliath's face . . . just about where Sterling hit it, too. I frown.

"Well," I say, "I tried." And when it comes to being remembered as we are, that's all any of us can do, right?

Dad snorts, already pulling his metal canteen out of his bag. "We have plenty of stuff to throw at it," he says, launching the canteen like a football. It spirals through the air and hits the target with a satisfying metal *clink*.

"You did it!" I shout.

"But now what?" Liat asks.

We all look around, waiting. There's a rattle from Goliath's face, and then a grate falls down, covering the water sluice. The water below us starts to rise.

"I do not like where this is going," Sterling says.

"There has to be a reason for it," I say, though my voice sounds unsure.

The water hits the bottom of the platform we're standing on, and somehow, we start to rise with it. The platform is going up.

"What?" Gabe says. "How is water lifting stone?"

"I don't know," I say.

"Maybe it's not stone, just painted to look that way?" Liat says.

Dad raises a foot as if to stomp on it, but we all put our hands up. "No, Dad!"

"Henry!" Liat says at the same time.

Dad lowers his foot slowly.

"Look," Gabe says, pointing at the wall as we rise. A few thin lines are carved in it. The platform is being raised on grooves.

I lean toward the wall, listening. "More clockwork, I think. The water must be powering it somehow."

"Clever," Liat says.

"And a dramatic exit for after an initiation," Dad says.

We all look up, wondering where the platform is taking us. It's only about thirty more feet before the platform stops with a *thunk* and a splash. It's dark, but with our flashlights, we find we're just below one side of a small, plain room. The platform has stopped right next to a few stairs that lead up to the room's main floor. The water, though, keeps rising, stopping only when it's just below my knees. We all climb out and up the few stairs into the room. The only light comes from our flashlights, but there's nothing else to see. Just a door, a large wooden plank barricading it from the inside. Dad lifts the bar up and opens the door.

Outside is the village. It's quiet. We walk out onto the street, dripping wet from the knees down. I suddenly realize how tired

I am. I want to fall on the ground. But there's something more important than me. I open my backpack and check the lyre. Still dry in the bag and still intact. I actually have a chance to look at it now, even if it's only by the dim light of the stars and the few windows that are still lit.

The lyre is lighter than I thought it would be. And so simple. Wood, carved with a simple design of flowers, some metal at the top where the bar goes across it. There's a base, so it can stand on its own. It's inscribed with some Hebrew.

"'For my soulmate,'" Liat translates. "But be careful. We shouldn't touch it until we have gloves on. And have showered."

"Yeah," Dad says. "Hopefully there's a hotel still open."

"There is," Sterling says. "I made reservations in case." She takes out her phone, but it's dead. She sighs. "I think it was called La Coronne. I don't remember the address."

I take out my phone—in a waterproof case—and look it up. "It's just a few blocks," I say, forcing my heavy legs to start walking. "We're in an alley a few streets from where we went in."

When we get to the hotel, it's still open, one sleepy clerk at the desk, who, upon seeing us, immediately wakes up and shuffles us outside so we don't drip on the carpeting. After checking we do have reservations, he brings us towels, makes us dry off, and then shows us the service entrance. Thankfully we're on the ground floor, and the hallway is wood, so he wipes the floor as he herds us to our rooms, mumbling in French.

"He thinks we swam here," Gabe says. "Sounds like it happens sometimes."

"Tourists," the clerk says, sounding more exhausted than me.

In our rooms, I put the lyre aside and shower. Afterward, we all gather in Dad's room and put on gloves to finally look at it while Sterling films.

"It's so plain," Liat says, her eyes wide. "How did the strings survive so many years? Do you think it's been restrung?"

"I don't know," Dad says. "It's in great shape, though. They're going to want to carbon-date it to prove it's really as old as David and Jonathan."

"I thought I heard it rattle before," I say. "Is anything loose?"

Liat slowly rotates it and turns it over. "There's a compartment in the base." She shows us. A simple latch keeps it closed. She opens it, and inside is a piece of wood, which she takes out. Sterling gets close to film it. It's carved and polished, a wooden note in Hebrew with some symbols underneath that I don't understand.

"It says 'For Jonathan,'" Liat says.

"Another puzzle?" Dad asks.

"It's music," Gabe says. "It's a melody for the lyre."

Liat looks at him. "How can you tell that?"

"I know music," Gabe says with a shrug. "The notation isn't identical, but I can still see . . . the pattern in it. And I've been studying the lyre. Not this lyre, I mean, but, like, generally how to play lyres. So I probably could, if you want."

Liat looks uncertain.

"Imagine if we can include footage of him playing it in the exhibit," I say, nodding at Sterling. "That would be something, right?"

"It would," Dad says. "And he's wearing gloves."

"All right, but be careful," Liat says, handing Gabe the lyre. "Those strings will probably snap the moment you try plucking one."

"I'll be careful," he says. "Show me the music."

She holds it in front of him, and he stares at it, his fingers moving near but not yet on the strings as he practices. Sterling backs up, filming.

Gabe takes a deep breath, then nods and begins playing.

I'm not someone who knows much about music. I know what I like, but I couldn't tell you what makes a song good or bad to me. All I know is the music is beautiful. A little sad, but mostly it's . . . love, somehow. It fills the room, and I feel like I know the player is in love—not brotherly love, not friendship love, but real romantic love. The kind they write epics about, the kind of big love you see in movies or Shakespeare plays. It swells inside me, like my blood is humming along with the melody, and it makes me feel like I'm in love, too. My heart races, my skin tingles. The music makes me shimmer.

And there's more than just romance in the song. It's a story—the swell of falling in love and finding yourself with someone else alongside you. It's knowing how someone can change you for the better. It's knowing that your story and theirs are linked now, and that it's still yours. People might try to tell it from the outside, but no one else can feel what it is to be a part of this love, this music, except by experiencing it.

My throat feels soft, shaky, and I realize I'm crying. I look around, and so is everyone else, even Gabe, who's still playing as tears fall down his face. As the final note ends, it quivers in the air for a moment. My whole body is covered in chills until the sound finally fades to silence.

And then, suddenly, in front of us, all the strings on the lyre turn to dust and blow away in spirals, even though there's no breeze.

We're all quiet.

"I'm sorry," Sterling says suddenly. "I . . . never really believed in all this. I mean, the lyre, sure, but David and Jonathan being lovers . . . I never believed it. Until now. That music . . . that was love." She sniffs and wipes her eyes.

"They'll have to play it at the exhibit," Liat says, taking out a tissue and wiping away her tears. "You got it on camera, right?"

"Yes," Sterling says.

Dad blows his nose loudly. "A really good find, Tenny," he says. "Important."

"I hope so."

"Let's maybe not show when all the strings turned to dust at once, though," he says to Sterling.

"Was it magic?" she asks.

Dad shrugs.

"I think the lyre just knew it needed to play that song again," Gabe says. "It's like it was guiding me."

"Jonathan died in David's war," I say. "David wept when he was told. I wonder if he wrote this after that."

"Maybe the carbon dating will tell us," Dad says. "We still have a lot to learn."

"Let the scientists do that," Liat says. "We found the lyre. Our mission is done. I'll let the USJHA know."

"And I want to sleep," I say.

"Okay," Dad says. "I'll go out and see if there's a store still open where I can buy a hard case for the lyre, maybe cut some foam to fit it so it's as safe as it can be."

"You should sleep, too," I say.

"We should all sleep," Liat says. "We will. Soon. Go get some rest, you two."

I smile at her, and Gabe and I go back to our room, where we fall into bed and sleep with the music still ringing in our ears.

By morning, Dad has managed to put together a safe case for the lyre. It's not perfect, but it's better than a padded envelope. Liat has heard back from USJHA. The organization is excited to begin preparing the exhibit. There are researchers studying the photos she sent already, and they love the idea of playing this song, too. They're also excited for me and Dad to tour with the exhibit—as much as school allows. I'll be at the official unveiling of the lyre at the Jewish Museum in New York. Liat volunteered me to give some opening remarks. Sterling wants to time it so the exhibit opens at the same time that the show airs. Everything is falling into place. And I'm done.

We wait by the stairs leaving the mont, watching the water recede. There's a bunch of tourists with us again, some of them the same people who came with us yesterday. No one asks about Eriksen. I don't think anyone even knows he's missing yet. I'm not sure whose job it is to tell someone he died. Or that his hired muscle did, too. They might have families, and there's the Vatican. But what do I say? *They fell into a trap in front of us, and we couldn't save them?*

Dad looks down at me, and it's like he can sense what I'm thinking. "I'll reach out to someone I know who knows people at the Vatican, and we'll tell them. Someone will let them know. It wasn't our fault, Tenny. We couldn't have done anything."

"I know," I say.

When the water finally falls back from the shore, the sun is high and casts a bright light down on the path back to the mainland. The wet sand gleams like a mirror as we walk across it, and it's already getting hot enough that my neck starts to sweat. I'm barefoot again, the wet sand squeezing through my toes, making me feel grounded, part of the earth again. The music still lingers in my brain, though. I'll have to turn it into something I can just play on my phone. It'll fill me with pride, too, I think. Love and passion and sadness, but pride. The music of our history.

David always wanted the crown. That's something most historians agree on. Some say he was destined for it, but he definitely pursued it, even mounting a war against Saul, Jonathan's father. Jonathan took his father's side and died in battle. I don't know if David knew that would happen, but he had to suspect it. He lost Jonathan but gained the crown, and with it, he became a part of history that no one has forgotten. He tried to control his own story. But did he?

Tonight we'll fly back to New York. Liat will drop off the lyre. Sterling will start editing the footage with Dad. And I'll go back to my summer break, whatever that is.

"So, I feel sort of, like . . . now what?" Gabe says, walking next to me. "Is that normal? Just a comedown?"

"Yeah," I say, smiling. "I feel it, too. Did you like your first adventure, though?"

He nods. "It was . . . everything." He holds up his still-bandaged hand. "And I got a cool scar. Boys will love that, right?"

"Oh, you just wanted a good story to tell boys, huh?" I ask.

He laughs. "Yes. That's it exactly." We walk in silence a little longer. "But, really, thank you, Ten. I mean, I wanted to do it because it sounded so cool, and you always look so sweet on the show. And it was wild. Harder than I thought . . . scarier . . . but . . . also awesome."

"Life still all planned out?" I ask.

He smiles and looks up, the light hitting his face, or maybe he just lights up like that when he smiles. "Yeah . . . but . . . I feel like maybe adventure is part of it, too. Like maybe something unexpected could still happen."

"I think . . . when I was looking at those wheels back in Paris, I was thinking of David and the way we take pieces of history, look at pieces of people, and sort of assemble them to tell a story. We do it with history, and people do it with the pieces of me online . . . but we're bigger than those pieces. David was, too. And I think your future . . . you're looking at all these pieces laid out. But it's more than that."

He walks quietly for a moment, then nods. "We're all bigger than the pieces of us—future and past?"

"Yeah. Future is history, too, or it will be."

"I never thought I'd get to be a part of history, before. But now I feel like maybe I am."

"You were always a part of history," I say. "All of us are."

Gabe smiles at that, looks out at where the path starts on solid ground again. "I guess . . . we are," he says finally.

Dad upgrades us all to first class at the airport, and we can use the lounge. It's quiet and fancy, with a juice bar, waitstaff, and even little private rooms, which we all relax in.

"So," Sterling says, turning to me and taking out her camera, "I got the script from Thrill."

"Already?" I ask, feeling a sudden pit of dread in my stomach.

Sterling nods. "I also spoke to the network last night. They were . . . less enthusiastic than I hoped they'd be about us retrieving the lyre."

Dad frowns at that. "So we really are maybe getting canceled."

"But if you do this live ad for Thrill, I can make sure the money is earmarked only for us because it's through your advertising," Sterling says. "It's not a huge amount, but with everything else they're giving us, I think I can convince the marketing and publicity departments to make sure we actually get some ads, some posters, maybe they try calling some magazines . . . I can't promise it'll fix everything. But I think if we make a really great season—and with what we have, we can—then that little bit will be enough. Maybe not enough to get you on the cover of *Out*, but enough to make the network realize they shouldn't cancel you. I hope."

I sigh. "I almost wish we were still just doing it for the old network, just putting it together ourselves. It was easier."

Sterling nods. "I get that. But you have so much potential here. A bigger audience. Maybe. But doing the ad will help us out a lot."

I take a deep breath. "Okay."

Sterling lights up. "Thank you. We can do it right now if you want! Just put some of the lotion next to you, and I have the script here, let me email it to you . . ."

"Okay," I say. "But . . . just the two of us, okay? Dad, Gabe, Liat, can you . . . not be in this room?"

"I want to stretch my legs, anyway," Liat says, standing. "Have fun." She winks and leaves. Gabe squeezes my hand before he and my dad walk out, too. I pull up my phone and read over the script.

Hey, girls, gays, and all other ways. It's me, Tennessee, queer teen archaeologist. I'm on an adventure right now, finding an amazing new artifact, but I want to tell you about my best latest discovery: Thrill. They have this new line of skincare—sunscreen, hand cream, lip balm, all this good stuff. I've been using it all season while exploring ancient tombs and searching for lost queer treasure, and it works so great. Look how smooth my hands are! And my lips are soft, too, which is fantastic, because my boyfriend, Gabe, came along with me on this season, so keeping my lips soft has been pretty important, if you know what I mean. Plus it all smells so good! Sure, Thrill is a sponsor, but I would never talk up a product I didn't genuinely love. So you should totally try some. You can even use code "Tennessee" at ThrillLooks.com for 10 percent off a skincare starter kit! So check it out, and be sure to keep watching us explore history, ruins, and LGBTQIA-plus history, because love is love, and we love all of you!

I sigh. Reading it makes me queasy. But we need the money for marketing if I want queer history marketed, right?

1. Do the script as written. Die inside.
2. Don't do it, lose the money, and probably lose the show.
3. Maybe do it . . . but do it right. Thrill really did help me out, after all. And I don't mind the products. I just don't want to be a symbol. A human-size, happy "love is love" emoji for them to slap on their stuff. I'm a person. I'm complicated. Maybe if they want to use me as a symbol, they should use all of me.

"I think . . ." I push my phone to her. "I'm ready."

"You memorized it already?"

"Does it have to be word for word?"

"Well . . . no. But the basic idea . . . you have that?"

I nod.

"And you really want to do this? You have a funny expression."

I make myself smile. "For the show," I say.

She nods, excited, then takes out a little tripod and puts my phone on it. She clicks a few things and sets it facing me. I take out some Thrill products and put them around me on the table I'm sitting at. The background is nice—it's luxurious, fancy, like an ad should be. I wonder if Sterling saw that, which is why she's mentioning the ad now. I wonder if she'll talk to me after this. I don't . . . dislike her. She's been doing her job. It's not really her fault that this is what we have to do now. That the way we remember pieces of people and history is flat, uncomplicated. That we never look at pieces and know there's a bigger whole.

"Okay," I say. "I'm ready."

Sterling nods and counts down with her fingers. I look up at the screen as we go live, and I smile.

"Hi," I say. "So, this is totally a promoted thing. Thrill has this line of sunscreen and lip balm and hand lotion, and they asked me to talk about how nice it is, and yeah, it's nice. It smells good, and, like, I haven't gotten a sunburn on this trip, and I haven't broken out or anything. I'm not an expert. I don't really know."

Behind the camera, Sterling frowns.

"But let me tell you what I do know: this season, we went after a historical relic—and found it. One that's going to be controversial. The lyre that Jonathan gave to King David. Like David-and-Goliath King David. From the Bible. And I know a lot of people are going to take issue with that. Maybe you're already thinking, 'That's not queer,' because that's not the story you've heard."

I stop and take a breath. This is scary. This next part is what I want to say to Sterling—to the world—and I'm saying it, and I don't know if it will mean the end of the show. "I understand why you might think that. As a queer teen—a queer person—it often feels like people don't know my real story. Like, I do my historical TikToks and posts or put up a photo, and the comments are all over the place. There's the homophobia, of course—not my fave—but easy to ignore, to just hit block. But then there's also people saying my friend Gabe and I are such a cute couple—we're just friends, by the way—and that it's so nice to see gay love. Love is love! Rainbow emoji."

I sigh. Sterling is still filming, but she looks nervous. Her hand is inching toward the OFF button, but I shake my head. I have to say this. This is me taking control of my own history for once. I won't be like David.

I look up at the camera, smile. "And that's not bad! I love the support. I really do. But there's more to me than the narrative you've created in your heads." I nod, finally getting to what I want to say, and suddenly it's like I can hear David's song in my head again. That true expression of who he was. "I think about that a lot with history, too. With queer people in history. How we see only these little pieces of historical figures, and we try to create a story from them. It's why so many people in history are assumed to be straight, like David, even when there are convincing arguments that they weren't. The fragments of people we try to build a whole out of—whether those fragments are historical texts or social media—they don't tell a complete story. People make assumptions, and over time those assumptions become the official record. That's why it's important, I think, for us to try to control that official record with authenticity and honesty. Otherwise, people will take these pieces of you—whether that's queer, teen, archaeologist, or king, giant slayer, hero—and try to rearrange them in a way that best suits the story they want to tell. But it's *your* story. It's *our* history."

I almost laugh. It feels so good to finally say it to the world, to tell them that who they see me as is just as fake and poorly assembled as how most people see David. "So yeah, I've been thinking about that while researching this story of King David, looking for his lyre. Yes, David has kids with women, and yes, there's the story of him lusting after Bathsheba, but there's also the story of him and Jonathan, their love for each other, and I think that the fragments we have of that— and the ones we found while searching for the lyre—I think they can be arranged to tell a love story. A queer love story. And lots of people will tell you I'm wrong. They'll reorganize the pieces in the way they want them: straight. But I know I'm not wrong. I know queer love when I see it, and I think you will, too, when you tune in."

Sterling holds up a tube of Thrill sunscreen behind the camera, and I laugh. I said what I wanted, so now back to what she wants. Maybe it'll save the show—maybe not. But at least I've said what's important. "But back to the sponsored thing. Thrill. I've never met anyone from Thrill. They reached out to my producer, or my producer reached out them, I'm not sure, and they gave us a bunch of their products and asked us to use them on camera. Like I said, I like the products. Gabe really likes the way they smell, too. But I'm not a skincare expert." Sterling frowns, and I shake my head. "My producer is not happy I just said that. But the products really do smell nice. I like them, which I think is how an endorsement should sound, right?" I look at Sterling, who sighs, then look back to the camera.

"But let me say this: I don't know what fragments of me Thrill wants to use as advertising. I know they use trans models and have given to queer charities, which is amazing. I don't know if that's just for advertising, because they want queer money, though." Sterling looks genuinely angry, and her finger is moving to shut this down. "But," I say quickly, raising my hand, almost pointing at the camera, "they sponsored me. And this is an ad—not the ad they wanted, but still an ad for them. And I just want to say that if they're willing to accept every piece of me"—I put my hand over my chest—"every fragment, not just 'love is love' and rainbow emojis, but the part where I'm out here saying

King David was queer, which we all know will be controversial . . . If they support all that . . . then I don't think it's just corporate." Sterling looks surprised but happy. "And they've known all season what I've been looking for. So I think they do support it. They support not just every piece of me, but every piece of queerness in King David. And that's kind of huge." I look at the camera and nod, smiling. "So, thank you, Thrill. Like I said, I don't know skincare, but I like their stuff." I laugh. "Also, the hand cream literally saved the day at one point. But I'm not going to spoil that for you; you'll have to watch the season."

Sterling moves to turn the camera off, but I shake my head. "And I just also want to say that I don't know what happens next. The new network we're on—they didn't love my going after King David's lyre. They might cancel us, and we'd have to take some time off and then maybe upload our own stuff on the Internet or something . . . I don't know. So maybe this season is the last you'll see of me and my adventures for a while. But even if you don't see me out there, searching for queer history, just know that I still am. And you still can be, too. It's your history. And every time someone tries to tell you, 'There were no queer people in ancient wherever,' you can fight that. You can prove them wrong. That's something all historians should start considering."

I pause for a moment and look at the tube of sunscreen. I don't know what Thrill is going to make of this. I don't know what comes next. Maybe the show ends here. But we found the lyre, and it's going on tour with a love song about two men from the Bible. And that's something. That's something that'll show anyone who sees it who we are and how we've always been there. That we're all a part of history, like I told Gabe. And that's what's most important.

"And hey," I say to the camera, just in case, "if this is the last season for a while, I just want to say you are all amazing. Thank you for watching. And never forget: we're all a part of history. And because of that, history is ours to make."

AUTHOR'S NOTE

History is what we make it.

Well, that's not entirely true. But it's what we make of the pieces we find. I am well aware I will get hate mail for this book; I will be called a liar. So let me lay out what is real and what isn't: First off, the lyre isn't real. The secret society isn't real (at least, I don't know if it is), and many of the specific locations—the churches, etc.—are not real. Even the mont is made up, though heavily inspired by Mont-Saint-Michel.

But Jonathan and David being in love I did not make up. The fact that David and Jonathan's love is a specific word for love used elsewhere for married couples and God is true. The stripping naked to proclaim devotion is in the Bible. Translations often give you "Jonathan Loved David with his whole soul" or "more than a woman." It's all there if you put the pieces together. I genuinely believe that David and Jonathan were lovers—as do many Bible and Torah scholars. I read numerous essays and a few books on the subject while writing this novel, research all about David and Jonathan and the way queerness was treated in ancient Judaism. The most notable of these I mentioned in the book: *Jonathan Loved David* by Tom Horner, which lays out the argument carefully and precisely using translation of language and comparison to other biblical sections. That key text led me to read from the works of John Boswell, Martti Nissinen, and various other theologians. But if you want a core text to read, start with the Horner.

History aside, I have many people to thank for this book making it out there. It's been a long road, but thankfully I haven't had to tread it alone. I've had two editors, Suzy and Abby, by my side, both of whom brought me fantastic guidance. Thank you, both. My agent, Joy, who is family and has been with me for so long that she knows exactly what she needs for me and from me and makes everything so much smoother. Thank you, Joy. And thank you to my fantastic publicist, Jenny, assistant editor, Stefanie, and copyeditor, Kayla, and the whole team at Union Square.

Thank you to Colin, my cover artist, one of the most talented people I know, who also does the covers of my Evander Mills books! I'm so glad we get to conspire on so much together.

And thank you to all my writing buddies who keep me as close to sane as I can be in this madhouse of a career: Dahlia, who was also my "Am I Hebrew-ing right?" consultant, and Cory, Gus, Adam, Sandy, Caleb, Cale, Adib, Julian, Robin, Laura, Dan, and Jesse, and so many others.

And to Chris for being Chris.

ABOUT THE AUTHOR

L. C. Rosen writes books for people of all ages, including the Evander Mills series, which began with the Macavity Award–winning *Lavender House* and continues with *The Bell in the Fog*, and *Rough Pages*. His most recent YA novels are *Emmett* (Best Book of the year from *Kirkus Reviews* and Amazon), *Lion's Legacy* (Best Book of the year from *Booklist* and the New York Public Library), and *Camp* (Best Book of the year from *Forbes*, *Elle*, and the *Today* show, and others). He lives in NYC with his husband and a very small cat. You can find him online at LevACRosen.com and @LevACRosen.